Grimm's
most famous fairy tales

Grimm's
most famous fairy tales

REBO
PRODUCTIONS

©   1997 Rebo Productions Ltd.

adaptation text: Rindert K. de Groot
illustrations: Gris di Luca
cover design: Ton Wienbelt, Den Haag
production: TextCase, Groningen
typesetting and layout: Michele Thurnim, TextCase
translation: First Edition Translators Ltd, Great Britain

ISBN 1 901094 06 5

Contents

The Goosegirl

nce upon a time there was an old queen who had a very beautiful daughter. The queen's husband, the old king, had died many years before while his daughter was still very small, but the princess did not miss her father too much, for she and her mother lived very happily together.

When the princess grew up, she met a prince from a country far away. The two of them liked each other so much that they decided to be married, but the princess stayed with her mother a little longer. She wanted time to pack her belongings at her leisure, taking everything she would need when she went to marry the prince in his country far away. At last the time came for the princess to travel to that distant land and be married, and the old queen gave her a great many magnificent clothes and jewels, besides gold and silver, goblets and ornaments. A lady in waiting was to be the princess's companion on the journey, and place her hand in the prince's on their wedding day.

They each had a horse to ride. The lady in waiting's mount was an ordinary animal, quite well mannered and strong, but not very handsome. However, the princess's horse was a beautiful creature who could gallop like the wind. He was called Falada, and there was something else very unusual about him: he could speak human language.

When the princess had finished her packing, had her cloak on and was waiting to say goodbye to her mother, the old queen went to her bedroom and made a little cut in her finger with a sharp knife, so that it bled. She put a white cambric handkerchief under the cut and let three drops of blood fall on it. Giving her daughter the handkerchief, she told her, "Dear child, always keep this with you. It will be useful on your journey." Then they said goodbye to each other, and although the princess was looking forward to going to her prince's country, she wished that her mother could go too, so she was rather sad, and there were great tears in her eyes as she mounted the horse Falada.

After the two young women had been riding for a while, the princess felt very thirsty, and she said to her lady in waiting, "Take my goblet and

fetch me some water from the river. I can't ride any further without a drink."

"If you're thirsty," said the lady in waiting, "dismount from your horse, kneel down by the water's edge and drink. I'm not your maidservant!"

She spoke roughly, but the princess did not want to quarrel, and she dismounted from her horse. As the lady in waiting would not give her the golden goblet, she bent down to the river and drank from her hands. She did not mind that, but she did mind the lady in waiting's disobedience, and as she drank the water from the river she sighed, "Alas!" And the drops of blood on her old mother's cambric handkerchief answered her, saying, "If your mother only knew, her heart would surely break in two!"

The princess was a good, kind girl, who did not like to be angry or quarrel with anyone, so she said nothing, but mounted her horse once more. They rode some way further, but it was a hot day, the sun burned down, and the princess felt thirsty again.

When they came to another river, she said to her lady in waiting, "Get down from your horse and fetch me some water in my golden goblet!" By now she had forgotten how roughly the lady in waiting had spoken to

her. But the lady in waiting said, even more disagreeably than before, "If you want water, get it yourself. I'm sure I am not your maidservant."

Well, the princess was very thirsty, so she dismounted and bent down by the water as it flowed past. She shed tears and said, "Alas!", and the drops of blood answered her. "If your mother only knew, her heart would surely break in two."

As she leaned over the water to drink, the cambric handkerchief with the drops of blood on it fell out of her dress and drifted away downstream, but the princess was so tired and hot that she never noticed. However, the wicked lady in waiting had seen what happened, and she was very glad of it, because she knew the handkerchief was a magic one. Now that the princess had lost the three drops of blood on the piece of cambric, the lady in waiting could be mistress instead of her, for the princess suddenly felt tired to death.

The princess was about to mount her horse Falada again, but the lady in waiting said, "Falada is mine now. This old horse will be good enough for you!" So the lady in waiting gave the princess her own horse, and took the magnificent steed Falada for herself.

The poor little princess was forced to do as she said, and the lady in waiting was not satisfied yet. She made the princess take off her beautiful clothes, and put them on herself, while the princess had to wear the lady in waiting's dress. Then the princess had to promise never to tell a living soul what had happened, and if she had not given her promise she would have been killed on the spot. However, her horse Falada saw and heard everything, and remembered it well.

Finally the lady in waiting mounted Falada, the poor bride mounted the old horse, and so they went on their way.

There was great rejoicing when at last they reached the castle. The prince made haste to meet them and lifted the lady in waiting down from her horse, thinking she was his bride. So she was led upstairs, while the real princess had to stay below and wait in the courtyard until her mistress sent for her. How could everyone believe that the lady in waiting was the princess? The princess did not understand it at all, but she was too weary and felt too wretched to do anything about it.

Now the old king, the prince's father, looked out of his window and saw the pretty, delicate girl standing in the courtyard. He went to the bride's

room and asked what was to be done with her. Wasn't she the princess's lady in waiting, he asked? Who she was, and what was her name?

"Oh," said the wicked woman, "that's not my lady in waiting. She's just a girl I met on the way and brought along for company. Give her some work to do to keep her out of mischief." However, the old king had no work for her, and he could think of none either, so in the end he said, "I have a boy who herds the geese, and she can help him."

The boy's name was Conrad, and the real bride was sent to help him look after the geese.

A little later the false bride, who was really only the lady in waiting, asked the prince, "Dear bridegroom, will you do something for my sake?"

"Yes, to be sure," he said.

"Then will you ask the knacker to slaughter the horse I rode on my way here? I had a great deal of trouble with him on the journey, and I won't ride him any more. He bites and kicks, and soon he'll do someone harm, so he had better be slaughtered."

However, the wicked lady in waiting was really afraid the horse might speak and say what she had done to the princess. She did not tell the prince that, and so it was decided that poor, faithful Falada must die. When the true princess heard of this she promised the knacker a piece of gold if he would do something for her. There was a great, dark gateway on the outskirts of the town, and she had to walk through this gate every morning and every evening with the geese.

"Will you nail Falada's head up there," she asked, "so that I can see it as I pass that way?"

The knacker thought this a strange request, but he liked the girl, so he promised to do as she asked, and when he had cut off the horse's head he nailed it up over the dark gateway.

Early in the morning, when the real princess went through the gate, she said as she passed by:

Alas, Falada, you hang there.

And the head answered her:

Alas, princess, and you walk there.
If your mother only knew
Her heart would surely break in two.

Then she went on out of the town and into the field with the geese, and on the way she talked to the gooseherd, whose name was Conrad. When they were out in the fields the princess sat down in the grass and

loosened her hair. It gleamed like pure gold, and Conrad, seeing it, thought it was so beautiful that he tried to pluck out a few hairs, but she said:

Wind, wind, blow today,
blow Conrad's hat away!
Make the boy run after it.
In the meantime here I'll sit
combing out my hair and then
pinning it all up again.

Immediately a brisk wind rose and blew Conrad's hat far away over the fields, so that he had to run after it. By the time he came back, the princess had combed out her hair and braided it so neatly that he couldn't pluck out a single hair. He was angry, and said no more to her, and they herded the geese until it was evening and time to go home.

Next morning, as the princess went through the gateway, she said again:

Alas, Falada, you hang there.

And the head answered her:

Alas, princess, and you walk there.
If your mother only knew
Her heart would surely break in two.

Once again, when they came to the fields, the princess loosened her hair and began to comb it out. Conrad came running up to pluck a few of her hairs out, but she quickly said:

Wind, wind, blow today,
blow Conrad's hat away!
Make the boy run after it.
In the meantime here I'll sit
combing out my hair and then
pinning it all up again.

Then the wind rose again and blew Conrad's hat far away over the fields, and once more he had to run after it. When he came back all her hair was neatly plaited into a long braid, and he couldn't pluck out a single hair from her head. So once again the two of them herded the geese until evening.

When they were home, Conrad went to the old king and said, "I don't want to herd geese with that girl any more."

"Why not?" asked the king.

"Because she torments me all day long!"

The old king asked what she did, and Conrad said, "When we go through the dark gateway in the morning, she talks to a horse's head nailed up on the wall above it, and she says:

Alas, Falada, you hang there.

And then the head answers:

Alas, princess, and you walk there.
If your mother only knew
Her heart would surely break in two."

Then Conrad told the king what happened out in the meadow, and how he was made to run after his hat in the wind.

The old king told Conrad to go to work as usual the next day. But he wanted to find out the beautiful girl's secret for himself, so he went and stood behind the dark gateway, where no one could see him, and he heard the princess speak to Falada's head.

Then he went on into the fields, hid behind a bush and saw the goosegirl and the boy driving their geese along. After a while he saw the girl loosening her hair, which gleamed in the sunlight, and next moment she said:

> Wind, wind, blow today,
> blow Conrad's hat away!
> Make the boy run after it.
> In the meantime here I'll sit
> combing out my hair and then
> pinning it all up again.

Then there came a gust of wind which blew Conrad's hat away, and the boy had to run after it. While he was gone the girl combed out her hair

and plaited it into a long, golden braid. After the king had seen all this he slipped away unnoticed.

That evening, when the goosegirl came home, the old king summoned her and asked why she did all these things.

"I must not tell you," she said. "nor any living soul. I had to swear I wouldn't, and if I hadn't given my promise I would have lost my life."

The old king asked more questions, but she refused to answer them and he could get nothing out of her. At last he said, "If you won't tell me, then tell your story to the iron stove there," and he went out of the room. She went close to the stove, and then she began to weep and wail, pouring out her heart and saying, "Here I sit, abandoned by the whole world, and yet I am a princess! It was my wicked lady in waiting who treated me so badly. She made me take off my royal clothes and put them on herself; she even took my horse. Now everyone thinks she is a princess, and she will be married to my prince, while I must herd geese. If my mother only knew, her heart would surely break in two."

The old king was standing outside by the stovepipe, and he heard everything she said. Then he came back and led her away from the stove. He had royal clothes put on her, clothes fit for a princess, and

when he saw how lovely she looked in them he was so astonished that he could scarcely say a word.

Next the old king called for his son the prince, and told him he was about to marry the wrong bride – she was only a lady in waiting, and a wicked one too. The real bride was here, said the king, the girl who was thought to be a gooseherd.

The prince was enchanted by his new bride. Once he set eyes on his lovely princess again, he couldn't understand how he had failed to realize that the lady in waiting was not his bride at all. The young prince thought his real bride was so beautiful and good that he never tired of gazing at her. A great banquet was held, and all the prince's friends and the people who worked in the castle were invited.

The bridegroom sat at the head of the table, with the princess on one side of him and the lady in waiting on the other side. By now the lady in waiting was so sure her wicked plans had succeeded that she never noticed who was sitting next to the prince on his other side, nor did she recognize the princess in her glittering robes.

When they had eaten and drunk, and everyone was very merry, the old king asked the lady in waiting a riddle.

"What does someone who betrays his master deserve?" he asked, and he told a story of a wicked deed very like what the lady in waiting herself had done, although it wasn't quite the same.

The false bride said, "Someone who betrays his master deserves to do dirty work for the rest of his life, cleaning shoes or something unpleasant like that, and never be allowed to do anything else. He should never have any easier kind of work, and that would make him understand what a wicked thing he did." The stupid lady in waiting did not realize that the king knew all about her own wicked deeds.

"Then that will be your punishment," said the king, "and it will begin at once. You can start this minute, for all the shoes in the castle must be cleaned before the wedding. Go and get down to work, and in a little while I'll come and see if you're cleaning them properly!" And when every pair of shoes in the castle was cleaned the lady in waiting had to begin cleaning them all over again.

The young prince married his princess, and they lived happily ever after in his castle. Later on, of course, he became king, and no lady in waiting or any of the other castle servants ever tried to cheat the prince or princess again, for fear of having to clean shoes for the rest of their lives. And they could see what boring, nasty work that was by looking at the wicked lady in waiting, who never did anything else.

Hans in Luck

Hans went out into the wide world when he was just a boy. He didn't want to stay at home any more, for he hoped to have many adventures, and life with his mother was dull. Every day was just the same, and Hans was discontented, so off he went, whistling as he walked along the road, and soon he found a master who could do with a good sturdy boy. Hans was happy, for now he could earn money of his own and learn a trade from his master too.

And so he did. His master was a joiner, and he taught Hans all he knew. Soon Hans himself could make very good chairs, tables, chests and beds – any piece of furniture he liked.

When Hans had worked for his master seven years, he said, "Master, my time's up, and I'd like to go back to my mother. Will you give me my wages?"

"You've been a good, honest, faithful worker," replied his master, "so here's a good gold bar for you. You've earned it!"

The gold bar was heavy, but Hans put it in a sack, and he set off on his way home with the sack over his shoulder. He was trudging along the road when he saw a horseman riding merrily by. The sun was shining, and Hans felt as if his gold bar was getting heavier and heavier all the time.

"Oh," said Hans, "what a fine thing it must be to ride a horse like that! You sit at your ease as if you were in a chair, you don't stumble over the stones in your path, you don't wear your shoes out, and you get along faster too. And the best thing of all about riding a horse is that you don't have to carry anything heavy, because the horse does it for you!"

"Then why are you walking, silly boy?" the horseman asked him.

"I have no horse, sir," said Hans, "and I have to carry a gold bar home too! I can't walk straight, and my shoulder is sore. But there it is, I don't have a horse!"

"Why don't we exchange, then?" said the man. "My horse in return for your bar of gold! He's a good animal, and you won't lose by the deal! Then you can sit comfortably on his back, and I'll just buy another horse. I don't mind. I've been riding so long that I feel like walking a bit for a change!"
"Thank you!" said Hans. "But it's not a good bargain for you, you know. You'll have to carry that gold bar, and I know how heavy it is. However, I'm willing."

No sooner said than done. Hans climbed into the saddle and off he went, first at a trot and then at a gallop when he clicked his tongue as the horse's owner had told him to do. At first all went well, but after a while the horse began to miss his old master. It was all Hans's fault, thought the horse, and he would give Hans what he deserved!

Before he knew it, poor Hans was thrown out of the saddle and into the ditch. The horse wouldn't obey anyone but his old master. However, a farmer who was walking along the side of the road, taking his cow to be milked, managed to grab the horse by the bridle and bring him back to his new owner. Hans scrambled to his feet, looking very glum. This wasn't the idea at all!

"It looks as if you have to be a magician to ride a horse," said he. "Particularly a nag like this one, ripe for the circus! You're better off with that cow. I like her much better. She gives milk as well, and you can make it into butter and cheese! I'd give a good deal to have a cow like that!" "Then if you'd like her, why don't we exchange?" suggested the farmer. "This is a very fine cow, and she gives me a good bucket full of milk every day, so that I can make butter and cheese."

Hans agreed, and the man jumped on the horse and rode away like the wind. The cow stared stupidly at Hans, mooed once and looked the other way.

Hans was happy with his bargain, and he went cheerfully on, leading the cow along after him on a halter and thinking of the excellent deal he had done. I'll never die of hunger or thirst, he thought. Butter, cheese, milk … what could be more delicious?

This made him feel very hungry, so he stopped to rest at an inn, where he ate everything he had brought with him for his midday meal and his supper, and after that he ordered a bottle of wine to wash it all down.

His hunger was satisfied, his thirst quenched, and Hans went cheerfully on along the path. However, the sun was burning down, and it was getting hotter and hotter. Hans felt tired, but he had to go on. Early in the afternoon he came to a barren heath, and he knew he would have to walk for another hour before he could reach his home.

Then Hans decided to milk his cow and have a drink. He tied the cow to a tree, put his hat under her udder, and pulled one of the teats. However, nothing happened. He was so clumsy at milking that the cow lost patience and kicked him hard with her back feet. Hans fell to the ground, half stunned.

Luckily a butcher came along, wheeling a barrow with a fat piglet in it. "Hallo there, what's the matter with you, young fellow? You look very

pale. Have a drink and you'll feel better," he told Hans, helping him to his feet again.

Hans told the butcher what had happened to him.

"My poor boy," said the man, roaring with laughter, "this cow's an old animal, good for nothing now but to draw a cart or be taken to slaughter. You'll never be able to milk an old cow like that. You're only hurting the poor creature."

"Oh, dear me! I don't have any cart, and I don't like beef," replied Hans sadly. "I wish I had a fat pig like yours there instead. Just think of the juicy pork chops you'll get from it, and the delicious black pudding, and the wonderful sausages! I love to eat sausages. Just thinking of them makes my mouth water! What's more, pigs are cheerful animals, and at least a pig would give me something to laugh at. That cow just gapes stupidly at me and then gives me a nasty kick!"

"Would you like my pig in exchange for your cow?" asked the butcher. "I'm a kindly soul. I don't mind helping you out."

"That's very good of you," said Hans, giving him the cow, while the butcher turned the pig out of its barrow and gave Hans a rope to put around its neck.

So Hans went on again, leading the pig on its rope behind him, and thinking how well everything was turning out today, better than he could have hoped for.

A little further on he met a farm worker carrying a fine goose under his arm. They said good day to each other, and Hans struck up a conversation with the young man, telling him how lucky he had been with all the bargains he had struck.

The young man listened to Hans, and then he said he was taking his goose to an important gentleman who lived some way off. There was a christening party at the gentleman's house, and the goose was to be slaughtered and roasted.

"Just feel how heavy she is," he said. "She's been fattened up for at least eight weeks. The folk who eat this goose when she's all roasted and served up crisp and brown will be licking their fingers!"

"Yes, that's a fine bird," replied Hans, "but my pig's not so bad either!"

Suddenly the farm worker began looking uneasily around him, and then he said, "I'm afraid you may be in trouble with your pig. You certainly struck a bad bargain there, and you could end up in prison, because

that pig looks suspiciously like the pig stolen from the village mayor this morning. The mayor's servants are out looking for it. You'd better get rid of it! If they find you leading the mayor's pig around on a rope, then I can tell you you're in trouble!"

"Oh dear – please help me!" said poor Hans, terrified. "You're better known around here than I am. Take my pig in exchange for your goose!" "It's a pretty risky thing you're asking me to do, because of course I don't want to be caught red-handed with the mayor's pig either," said the farm worker, "but I wouldn't want you to go to prison. Very well, then, I agree!"

And he went off by a roundabout way, taking the pig with him.

Hans followed his own path, feeling relieved. "That's another good bargain I struck," he said to himself. "We can roast the goose, and eat its fat dripping on our bread. The dripping will last at least three months. And I can use the feathers to stuff a plump pillow and sleep on it. Oh, won't my mother be pleased!" And Hans went along the road, whistling

happily. He was coming closer and closer to his mother's village, so he was in a good temper.

A little later, Hans came to a village where a knife grinder was standing in the village square, turning his grindstone and singing:

Come up, good folk, in a crowd or alone,
and I'll sharpen your scissors and knives on my stone.

"You must be doing good business," said Hans, "or you wouldn't be singing so merrily!"

"That's right, my lad, business is certainly good!" said the knife grinder. "I earn well in this job. A good knife grinder always has money in his pocket. Oh, what a fine goose you have there! Where did you buy it?"

"I exchanged it for a fat pig. I had the pig in exchange for a beautiful cow, and the cow in exchange for a spirited horse, and the horse in exchange for a heavy gold bar."

"And what about the gold bar?"

"I had that as wages for my seven years' work," said Hans.

"Did you, indeed? Well, I see you know how to take care of yourself!" said the knife grinder, laughing. "If you only had money in your pocket, you'd be the luckiest man in the world!"

"But how can I get money in my pocket?" asked Hans.

"Why, become a knife grinder! Here, I'll give you this grindstone in exchange for your goose. The stone's a little damaged, to be sure, but it still works well enough. And I'll give you this big boulder too. You can

knock knives and other blades back into shape on it. Don't you think that's a good bargain? Earning money for yourself is a good notion, don't you agree?"

"I do, and I think you're quite right!" said Hans, giving the knife grinder his goose.

He hadn't gone a hundred yards before he felt worn out by the weight of the heavy stones he was carrying. Since he felt very thirsty, he stopped when he came to a well. He put the stones down on the side of the well, and bent over it to drink. However, he wasn't taking enough care, and by mistake he gave the stones a push, so that they fell to the bottom of the well with a great splash.

When he saw the stones disappear into the water, young Hans jumped for joy. He thanked heaven he was free of his heavy load at such a good moment. Now at least he didn't have to carry them any more. What luck! He was rid of them at exactly the right time.

"I'm the luckiest man in the world," he sang as he skipped along the path to his mother's house.

His mother was looking out for him, for she had an idea that Hans would come home some day. When she saw her son in the distance, she ran to meet him.

"How well you look, my boy!" she said. "And how you've grown! Well, how did you get on out in the world?"

Hans told her his story. He told her about his master, and how he had worked hard for seven years. Then he told her about the gold, the horse, the cow, the pig, the goose and the knife grinder. When at last he had finished his tale, his mother looked at him with tears in her eyes.

"My son," said she, putting her hand on his shoulder, "I always knew you'd grow up to be a fine, clever fellow. And now I hear your story I think you did very, very well. I'm really proud of you. I'm sure any mother would be glad to have such a good son. Come here and let me give you a big kiss!"

So they were both very happy, and Hans never went away again, but stayed at home and looked after his mother.

The Six Swans

Once upon a time there was a king who ruled his people strictly but justly. That wasn't always easy, for there were trouble-makers in his country who tried to cheat other folk and make a lot of money for themselves, which made the king feel sad, and tired too – tired because of all his anxieties. When it was very bad and he had to spend a great deal of time on the robbers and cheats he used to feel particularly gloomy, and wondered what was the use of trying so hard to make everyone in his country live happily and peacefully together. And when it was all too much for him, the king would go hunting to make himself feel better. He liked to be out of doors in the sunshine, seeing if he could bring down a pheasant or a rabbit, or even bigger game.

One morning the king woke very early, but he still felt very tired. He stretched, and thought he was so tired that he would like to spend another couple of hours asleep. The evening before he had been with his ministers until far into the night, talking about all kinds of important matters, and so he had stayed up much too late. The king climbed out of bed, sighing, and he immediately realized that he didn't feel up to ruling the country that day. So he decided to go hunting instead. He felt like a day of leisure, a day to enjoy being out of doors and riding his horse in the sun. Yes, that was what he would do, and then tomorrow he'd feel rested and fit to go on ruling his kingdom.

Soon he and his followers were riding out of the palace gardens, the king going in front on his magnificent horse, and his servants following him out into the great, wild forest that lay near the castle. The king had decided to hunt in a new place today. He had only just ridden into the forest when he saw an enormous deer among the bushes, a deer with antlers larger than any the king had ever seen before. The deer was as frightened of the king as the king himself was frightened of the deer. He stood there gazing at the splendid animal, and with one great bound it leaped out of the bushes and was gone.

The king spurred on his horse and gave chase to the frightened animal. The deer ran fast as the wind, and the king followed it fast as the wind too, indeed, he rode at such a pace that the rest of his companions soon lost sight of him. The servants' horses could not go as fast as the king's own horse, for of course he rode the swiftest, strongest horse in the whole country. None the less, his horse had difficulty keeping up with the deer, which was just as strong and swift. The hunt went on all day, and whenever the king drew near, the deer managed to escape just in time. In the end, when it began to grow dark, the king gave up his chase. He must be sure of getting out of the woods before night fell, or he could be hopelessly lost. The forest was so large that he did not by any means know his way all around it.

When he looked around him, however, he knew it was too late, and he had already lost his way. He was so far from his companions that he could no longer hear the music of the hunting horns, the crack of the guns and the shouts of the huntsmen. Moreover, he had reached a part of the forest where he had certainly never been before. He had no idea which way to ride to find his way back to his servants and his

castle. He tried bravely to find a way out, but here in the depths of the forest, where the tallest trees and thickest bushes grew, there were no roads or paths.

At last the king thought he must put up with spending the night in this forest. Or perhaps he needn't do so after all? For what was that among the bushes – did he see someone there among the trees? The king turned his horse in the direction of the place where he had seen something or someone moving, and found himself facing an old woman. She was a hideously ugly sight, with her wrinkled face and her long, untidy hair hanging in dirty tangles to her shoulders. Besides that, she had sly green eyes, a big hooked nose, and a mouth without a single tooth in it.

As soon as the king saw her he knew she was a witch, and he thought that odd, for many years ago he had made sure that all the witches in his land were captured. Obviously his soldiers had failed to find one of them, but as soon as he was back in his palace he would order them to track down this last witch, and then she could decide whether to stay in prison or go away to another country.

Just now, however, he was not in his castle with his soldiers, but here in the middle of an unknown forest, so the king pretended not to know what kind of creature stood before him, and in friendly tones he asked the woman to tell him the way.

Of course the witch had recognized him at once by the golden crown on his hat, and she said she would be happy to help his Majesty. "But you must do something for me too, your Majesty," she said. "And if you don't, you must spend the rest of your life wandering in this forest."

The king went scarlet with rage when he heard the witch make such bold conditions, but he hid his anger, and asked what she wanted.

"I'll tell you," said the witch, leering. "I have a daughter – and you won't find a lovelier girl in the world. She's so beautiful that she deserves to be your wife. Marry my daughter and make her queen, and I will show you the way back to the ordinary world and your castle."

Since the king did not intend to spend the rest of his life wandering around the forest, he agreed: very well, said he, he would marry the witch's daughter.

The witch went ahead of him to her little house, which lay hidden among the bushes. There was a strong smell in it of the strange potions brewed by the witch in an iron cauldron, which hung bubbling over the fire in a corner of the dirty room where she lived.

A girl was sitting beside the fire, and the witch had told nothing but the truth when she said her daughter was very beautiful. The girl was pretty as a picture, and yet the king saw at once that there was something the matter with her. Her eyes were green and sly, just like the witch her mother's.

32

But promises must be kept, and once you have promised you can't change your mind! So when the witch had shown the king the way, he put the girl on his horse in front of him. They rode almost all night long, and in the morning they came to the palace, where of course everyone had been in great anxiety about the king.

The royal servants had been up all night, and many of them had spent hours riding around the forest looking for their master. By now they were beginning to lose hope, fearing that he would never come back again.

That same morning the king sent messengers on horseback through the land, to announce that he was going to be married at once to the beautiful girl who had come to live in the palace with him.

Sure enough, a week later the wedding was celebrated with great magnificence, and the country had a queen again!

Again? Yes, again, for the king had been married before, but his wife, whom he had loved dearly, was dead. The king and queen had seven children at the time of her death: six sons and one daughter.

Of course the king loved his children very much, and since he was not entirely sure that their new stepmother would treat them well, he had them sent to a lonely castle which lay in the middle of a vast and almost impenetrable forest. It was a long way from his royal palace, and very few people knew it existed at all. Indeed, this castle was so well hidden, and the way there was so difficult to find, that the king himself could find it only with the aid of a good fairy. The fairy had given him a ball of yarn which had wonderful powers. When you rolled it ahead of you, it unwound of its own accord, knowing exactly where to go next, and led you to the place you wanted to find.

The king went to visit his children as often as he could. He enjoyed his visits very much, and so did the children, who were delighted whenever they saw him. Then they would play games together, and tell stories they had made up, and when the weather was fine they all went walking in the forest. The brothers used to make sure their sister did not stumble, and if she was tired one of them would carry her on his shoulders. All the boys were devoted to their sister, and she was devoted to them.

For some time all went well, and the king managed to visit his children frequently. But then the new queen began to think it odd that her

husband was away so often, and what was even worse, she thought, was the way he always looked so happy when he came back. Then, after a few days, he would grow sorrowful again, and he went away once more. The queen knew that the king liked to be out of doors in the sun, but after they were married he spent so much time out in the open that she was bound to notice.

"I wish I knew what he does in the forest," she said to herself discontentedly. "He doesn't go hunting, for he takes no gun with him, and besides, he never brings any game back to the palace. No, he has some other kind of business in the forest, and I must know what it is or I'll never rest!"

She asked the footmen and maidservants and grooms if they knew where the king went so often, but none of the servants would say. They respected the king, they had loved his first queen very much in the old days, and they all adored the king's seven children. If the king wanted to keep his children hidden from the new queen, they thought, he must have his reasons. Besides, they did not like the new queen at all, for she would speak harshly to the servants for the least little thing. So they all held their tongues – except for one!

That one was a footman who had once stolen something, The king found out, and the footman was severely punished. It was his own fault, of course, but all the same he still bore the king a grudge. And when the queen promised him a large sum of money if he would tell her where the king went so often, he decided to give the secret away. It would serve the king right for punishing him so harshly!

So he told the queen about the king's children, and the castle where they were living in hiding. He even told her the secret of the ball of magic yarn. Yet the footman still had some scruples, for he told the new queen about the king's six sons, but he never mentioned their sister. And so it was that the queen knew the king had six sons. She felt more and more curious, and began making wicked plans.
"I must find the ball of magic yarn first," thought the queen. "And find it I will, if I have to knock down this palace singlehanded, from the top of its towers to the deepest dungeons."
However, she didn't have to go to so much trouble, for one day, while the king was with his ministers and she was searching the bedroom

cupboards on the sly, she found what she was looking for, carefully hidden among the folds of the king's ermine cloak.

Now the queen set to work. She made six shirts of white silk, and as she had learned the black arts from her mother the witch, she sewed a little magic into every stitch.

Then the queen began looking for an opportunity to carry out her wicked plans in secret, for of course she didn't want the king to notice anything, and she waited impatiently, keeping watch on her husband.

At last her chance came. The king of the country just over the border invited her husband to a great festival, with hunting parties, a knightly tournament and other pleasant entertainments. That meant the king would be away for at least a few days, and she could get to work at her leisure. Of course she did not want to attend the festivities herself, so she told the king that she didn't feel very well and was rather tired, and she would prefer to stay at home to rest.

As soon as the king had left, she packed up the six white shirts and the ball of magic yarn and went into the forest. Once there, she rolled the ball of yarn ahead of her, and when the yarn unrolled itself she had

only to follow and it showed her the way to the hidden castle.

The king's children had seen someone coming in the distance, but they couldn't tell who it was through the thick bushes and the tall, densely growing trees. However, they thought it must be their father, since except for their servants he was the only one who knew where the castle lay.

So the boys ran happily to meet him, while the princess hurried to her room to put on her prettiest dress for her father.

Not until the very last moment did the boys see that they had made a terrible mistake, but by then it was too late! The new queen, who was a witch's daughter, after all, threw the white shirts over the boys' shoulders, and when the sixth and youngest prince felt the shirt touch him she changed all six of them into white swans, who rose into the air, flapping their wings, and flew away.

The queen laughed to herself. Now there would be an end of those mysterious visits to the forest! The thought made her so happy that she was better tempered than usual that day. She kept smiling all evening as she thought of the six princes' faces as they suddenly turned into swans. What a fine magic spell she had cast on them!

Next day, the king discovered that his sons had disappeared. He had left the other king's country in the morning, deciding to visit his children before he had to go back to his palace. But when he strode cheerfully into the castle, entered the hall and called out to let them know he had arrived, there was no reply. He called them by name, but still no one answered. All was quiet in the castle, except for the rustling of the leaves on the trees.

But then the king did see something: his daughter came slowly walking down the marble staircase of the castle, barely able to keep upright on her feet..

She was crying. Great tears trickled down her cheeks, and her eyes were red and swollen.

"What is it? Why are you alone? Where are your brothers?" asked the king, slowly beginning to realize that something terrible had happened.

"They … they've gone!" sobbed the girl. "They've gone away, but I don't know what happened. We … we thought you were coming, so they went to meet you, and then I saw my brothers suddenly change into swans, and at once the swans flew away!"

Now her tale was told, and very sadly the princess showed her father a few white feathers, dropped by the swans as they flapped their wings.

The king was very sad too. How could such a thing have happened? He had done his very best to take care of his children. A witch or a wizard must have wanted to harm him: there was no other explanation, for boys don't turn into swans of their own accord. However, it never occurred to the king that his own wife the queen had cast a spell on his sons, for even though she was a witch's daughter he had never seen her work any magic or enchantment, and besides, she still didn't know that he had any children.

So the king merely thought that he ought not to have been stupid enough to hide his children away in a great forest. He would have done better to keep them in his palace, where the new queen could have looked after them, and this would never have happened. The queen would have taken better care of his children than the servants, he thought. And now the king decided to take his little daughter back to the palace with him. He did not want any harm to come to her as well, and at home in the palace she would be safe.

Deep in her heart, however, the girl was afraid of the stepmother she had never seen. She didn't want to go with her father, and begged him to let her stay in the castle just for this one day and the next night.

When she made the king this request for the sixth time, with tears in her eyes, her father agreed. "Very well," he said, stroking her golden hair, "very well, but you are coming home tomorrow!"

As soon as the king had left, the princess packed a few things ready to leave the castle. "As long as that woman lives in my father's palace I will never go back to it," she said to herself, "but I will not stay here, for they would only come and take me away. I will go in search of my brothers."

She waited until it was quite dark, and everyone in the castle was asleep. Then she slipped out of her bedroom, creeping down the corridors and out of doors in her stockinged feet as quietly as she could. She walked all night. When day dawned she stopped to rest for a little on the banks of a lake, and then went on her way again. She walked for a day, a night and another day without resting much at all. Her feet were sore, she was hungry and thirsty, but she went bravely on.

Just as she was so tired that she could hardly put one foot in front of the other, she saw a little hut among the trees. She knocked at the door, but no one opened it. However, the door was not locked, so she went in. She found a bedroom with six beds made up. Although she was worn out, and felt she could sleep for weeks on end, she didn't like to get into one of the six beds. Instead, she crawled under one to sleep on the floor.

She fell asleep at once, and never even noticed that the floor was hard and cold. Then she was woken instantly by a strange sound. It was still dark and the sun had not yet risen, but she heard a rustling noise, the

40

sound of flapping wings. The princess was very frightened, and waking so suddenly, she was not sure where she was. She looked out from under the bed, and saw six white swans flying into the room one by one. They lay down side by side on the wooden floor and began to shed their feathers, blowing hard. Clouds of white feathers flew around, and once they had fallen to the floor in a great heap there stood the six princes, her brothers. The princess uttered a cry of delight and quickly crawled out from under the bed. How happy the princes were when they recognized their sister! They hugged her and kissed her, all of them laughing and talking at once. But their joy did not last long.

"You cannot stay here, dear sister," said the eldest prince. "This is not a huntsman's hut, but the home of six wicked robbers. If they find you here they will be sure to do you harm."

"But can't you protect me?" said the girl.

"That's the worst of it," replied one of the others, "we can't! We are powerless. Every morning we can shed our feathers and be your brothers again, but only for quarter of an hour, and then we turn back into swans."

Happy as she had been a moment ago to have found her brothers, the princess now began to weep. "Is there nothing I can do?" she sobbed. "Can't I do something to help you?"

"No, the conditions are too hard," said the brothers, as sad now as their sister. "The only way of breaking the spell would be for you to keep silent and say nothing, not a word, for six long years, nor must you ever laugh or even smile. Besides that, you must make each of us a shirt of white daisies. And even if you were to do all this, it would still be in vain if you so much as smiled at the last minute of the last hour of the last day of the last week of the last month of the last year. It's impossible, and besides ... "

But the princess never learned what else there was besides, for before the prince telling her all this had finished, the quarter of an hour was up, and her brothers flew away in the shape of swans, flapping their wings. However, the girl had made her decision. She would set her brothers free! She was afraid of the robbers who lived in the hut, so she quickly left the place and went further into the woods, finding shelter in a hollow tree when evening came.

Next morning she decided to stay there. If she must neither speak nor laugh, well, there was no one to speak to here, and she did not feel at all like laughing. However, there were plenty of berries growing nearby; she could pick the berries and eat them, and not far away ran a clear stream of water with a great many white daisies growing on its banks, the daisies she needed to make her brother's shirts.

She spent the first morning picking armfuls of daisies, and took them back to her shelter in the tree. When she had gathered some berries and had washed in the water of the stream, she set to work making the shirts which would turn her brothers back into real princes again.

She had no needle or thread, but she found a way to manage without: she carefully joined the flowers together by their stems. It was very slow work, but she had six years to do it, and you can fasten a great many daisy stalks together in six years.

So weeks, months, a whole year went by, and she lived there quietly alone, always working. All her days were the same: she picked berries, she washed in the stream, she gathered flowers and worked, never speaking a word, never smiling, not even when three tiny little woodfinch chicks hatched in a nest close to her hollow tree, and sat with their beaks gaping open for food all day long.

The animals who lived in the forest soon became used to the girl, for she kept very quiet and did none of them harm. None the less, they were amazed. What kind of strange girl was this who never said anything, never laughed, and worked all day long from early in the morning to late at night? Although they skipped and played to amuse her, she always looked a little sad.

Then, one day, something happened. The king of a country close to the forest went hunting in that part of it where the princess lived. When he came to the tree where the girl sat on a stout branch, working, he stopped and spoke to her.

"Who are you, and what are you doing here?" he asked. However, she only looked at him and shook her head, as if to say that she didn't understand. So the king asked her again, and then again, even trying a language spoken by the people of another country. But the answer was still the same: the princess shook her head and said nothing.

Some of the king's servants came up, and a few other men too, and one of them, a young fellow, called out, "If you won't come down of your own accord then I'll climb up and fetch you!" The princess wished very much that all these strange men would go away. What did they want? Money, perhaps, but she had none. Instead she threw down everything she had with her: her golden necklace, her rings and her bracelets. Still they did not go away, however, and now, even worse, the young man who had said he would fetch her down did indeed climb the tree, took her in his arms and carefully lowered her into the

outstretched hands of the others. They caught her and set her on the ground.

There she stood before the king, who said kindly, "Now, child, tell me who you are."

The girl looked gravely at him, her eyes wide, but she said not a word in answer.

"Do you live here in this tree?" the king went on, but still she did not answer. Perhaps she was mute and could not speak at all, thought the king. But she looked so sweet and lovely, and indeed she was so very beautiful, that he fell head over heels in love with her. He climbed down from his horse, put his cloak around her and set her on the horse in front of him. Then he mounted to the saddle again, and rode out of the forest with her, back to his kingdom and his palace.

Once they were there, the king told some of the ladies in waiting to dress the girl as finely as they could, so that everyone could see how lovely she was. She sat next to the king at supper that evening, and although he usually liked good food, he could hardly swallow a morsel today.

He could not keep his eyes off the princess either.

All of a sudden the king rose to his feet and said, "I have news for you and everyone else in the land, and very good news it is too. This very week I will marry the beautiful girl you see here beside me!"

Everyone sitting at the table was surprised. Why, the king had seen the girl for the first time only that afternoon! She was beautiful, to be sure, but who was she, where did she come from, and why did she never say a word?

The princess's own heart leaped with surprise and delight, for she had fallen in love with the kind and handsome king herself. But she remembered her brothers just in time: no smile came to her lips, and her mouth remained firmly closed.

After a few days of feasting, the king and the princess were married with great magnificence, and all the people in the land were glad to see their king happy with his lovely, silent bride.

All of them? No, not all; not quite everyone was happy. There was one person who did not like it in the least: the king's mother, a wicked, jealous woman, who took pleasure in harming others, and made trouble

whenever she had the chance. She liked nothing better than to set people at odds with one another.

"How could you marry a waif found in a tree?" she said angrily to her son. "You know nothing about her, not even her name! And you may think she can't speak, but I believe she fears you will ask her all kinds of questions and discover she's good for nothing, perhaps even a witch. Certainly she isn't worthy to marry a king!"

However, the king did not believe anything his mother said. He thought it a pity his bride never laughed or smiled or said a word, to be sure, but he loved her dearly, and he was delighted when after a year she bore him a child, a baby girl.

But his happiness was short-lived, for only a few nights after the baby's birth the king's mother, who was still angry with her son because of his marriage, went to the queen's bedroom. Very carefully and in secret, she stained the young queen's sheets with blood and stole the baby away.

Then she woke her son, crying out that he was married to a monster, a cannibal who had devoured her own child. "For look, the sheets of her bed are soaked in blood, and where's my grandchild?" asked the old queen. Of course the king did not know what had happened, but he read in his wife's eyes that she had not done what the old woman said. The king told his mother to stop saying such wicked things, for they were not true, and as for what had really happened, well, he would soon find out! However, he could discover nothing, hard as he tried, and the baby's disappearance was still a mystery when another child was born. This time it was a dear little boy, a prince!

The young queen did her best to take good care of her child. She kept watch on the baby day and night, for of course she knew what had happened to her little daughter, but although she knew, she could not tell anyone. However, she could not stay awake for ever. She was bound to fall asleep some time, and she needed sleep so badly that one night she did. The king's mother had been waiting for that, and she immediately took the little prince out of his cradle and stained the young queen's sheets with blood again. Once more the old woman told the king he must send away his queen, a wicked mother who had eaten her own children.

Once again, however, the king would not believe what his mother said. "My wife is too good and sweet and lovely to do anything wicked," was all he replied, "and if she could speak I am sure she could tell us what has happened."

Yet even though the king swore that his wife could have done no wrong, he became unhappier and unhappier. Servants went searching for his children all over the land, in every village, in every house, even in other countries – but they found nothing. The king would often sit staring sadly into the fire, and then he thought of his children, and wished he knew where they were. He did not talk much himself now, and every day there were a few more white hairs on his head.

The young queen saw it all, and she was very sorry, but there was nothing she could do. More and more often she shut herself up in a little room in one of the palace towers, and there she worked away as hard as she could on the shirts made of daisies. Every free minute she had, she fastened as many daisies as possible together by their stalks. For there was not much time left now before the six long, long years were over.

Then her third child was born, and whatever the king did to keep this baby, it too vanished without trace, except for the blood on the sheets of the queen's bed. Once again the king's old mother began accusing the queen, and this time many people began to think that she must be telling the truth: surely she was right, for where were the babies now? They could hardly just have disappeared.

One day so many people came to the king's palace that they filled the square outside it. And the whole crowd shouted for the queen who killed her own babies to be brought out. "Burn her at the stake!" cried the people at the tops of their voices. "We don't want her as our queen any more – burn her at the stake!"

Now the king had to listen to his people. Once again he begged his wife to tell him what had become of the children, but she shook her head and said nothing. He was sure his wife had done no harm, and kept trying to put off the moment when she must be burnt at the stake. And he did put it off a few times, but in the end soldiers came to take the queen away to the market place, where a great fire stood ready. When she was put in a cart between two tall soldiers, the king's mother

came up carrying a great pile of shirts made of daisies. "Here," she chuckled, "take these nasty shirts too. They'll burn nicely! That's all this fine lady has done here, making silly shirts that are no good to anyone." But she was wrong, for as the cart reached the market place and the soldiers put the young queen on the fire there was a sudden rushing noise in the air, the sound of six great white swans who came flying up. The queen took the shirts she had made and threw them over the swans – over the first swan, the second, the third, and at last over the sixth. However, the sixth shirt was not quite finished; there was still one sleeve missing.

As soon as the shirts slipped over the swans' heads a strange thing happened: instead of a swan, there stood a young man who immediately began treading out the fire. This happened six times, although the sixth transformation was not complete: since one sleeve was left unfinished, the last prince had a swan's wing where he ought to have had an arm, but he did not mind that, and went as fast as he could to help tread out the fire. The second prince took his sister in his arms, the third finished putting out the flames, and the people in the market place fell silent and stared and stared.

Then the queen went to her husband the king, put her arms around him and kissed him. "Now at last I can tell you everything," she said. "Now I can speak and explain it all. I am innocent. Your mother took our children away, and everything she said about me was a lie."
And she told the whole story: how she had not spoken or laughed for six years to save her brothers, and how much she loved the king her husband.

There were many changes in the palace after that. The king's old mother was forced to say where she was hiding the children who had

disappeared, and then she was shut up in a dungeon in the castle cellars, never to be set free again.

The king who was father of the six princes and the princess soon heard that his sons were back, and he came to visit his daughter in her palace.

Their stepmother had disappeared: at the very moment the six swans turned into princes again, she was changed into a thin puff of smoke and flew out of the chimney and away.

So they all lived happily ever after, the king and his queen and their children, and of course the children's six uncles and their kind old grandfather.

Hansel and Gretel

Long ago there were two children, a brother and a sister, who lived in a great forest. The boy was called Hansel and his sister's name was Gretel.

Hansel and Gretel were very happy with one another and their father and mother. Their father was a woodcutter who went to the forest every day looking for old wood, which he chopped into neat little pieces with his hatchet. In the evening he came home, and once a week he went to town to sell his wood. The money he earned from it bought the family everything they needed.

One day, however, life began to go wrong for Hansel and Gretel. Their mother fell sick. At first she was only a little unwell, but then she grew worse and worse, and at last she died. Hansel and Gretel were left alone with their father in the little house in the forest.

Soon, however, Hansel and Gretel had a new mother, for their father

married again and brought his new wife home to his house. He thought he couldn't manage without a wife, and Hansel and Gretel needed someone to look after them. It would be nice for the children to have a mother again, he thought, and so it was at first. But very soon everything changed.

The woodcutter's wife did not like children at all. She thought them nothing but a tiresome nuisance, and so she was often cross with them, even when they hadn't done anything naughty. And that was not all, for Hansel and Gretel's father could not find enough wood in the forest now. He spent longer and longer in search of wood, and went further and further from home, but still he couldn't find enough to sell. Every week, when he went to town, he came back with less money, every week there was less to eat on the table, and every day they all went to bed a little earlier, so that the stove could go out sooner and the candles need not burn so long.

One evening the woodcutter and his wife were in the bedroom, sighing over their sad fate. Hansel and Gretel were in bed already, and their parents thought they had fallen asleep long ago.

However, Hansel was not asleep. He heard everything his father and mother were saying to each other.

"What's to become of us?" said the woodcutter. "How are we to give our children enough to eat when we don't have enough ourselves?"

"I'll tell you what to do," replied his wife. "We'll take the children out into the woods with us, and after a while we'll leave them behind, deep in the forest. Then we'll be rid of them! We won't have to feed them any more, and that will make quite a difference."

At first the woodcutter refused to agree to this wicked plan, but the children's stepmother pressed him so hard that at last he sighed, "Very well, then. I don't know what else we can do."

When his parents had fallen asleep, Hansel slipped out of doors and filled his pockets with pebbles, and next day, when the children went out into the forest with their father and stepmother, he scattered the pebbles along the path.

They came to a clearing deep in the forest, and the woodcutter stopped and said, "Well, children, you just stay here and wait for me. I'm going a little further to chop some wood. I'll be back for you again very soon."

However, he was not back soon. Hansel and Gretel waited and waited, and Gretel was very sad.

"How will we ever find our way home again?" she said, shedding tears. "Father has forgotten us. He must be home by now, and we don't know the way!"

But Hansel knew the way. He had only to see where his pretty white

pebbles were scattered, and the two children could easily find their way back by following the trail. It was very late when they came home, but they made their way back at last.

Their stepmother had not expected to see them at all. She pretended to be very glad the children were home, and said she had been anxious, but in fact she was not pleased at all, for she wanted to be rid of them. Their father really was glad, because it had made him very sad to leave his children behind in the forest.

However, the woodcutter's wife wanted to try again, and although the woodcutter protested, and said he would work harder to find enough wood to sell, it was no good. Once again, the children had to go into the forest, but this time their stepmother locked the door the evening before they went, so that Hansel could not get out to collect pebbles.

Guessing her plan, however, Hansel had another trick up his sleeve. He took a hunk of stale bread out of the cupboard when no one was looking, and scattered breadcrumbs along the path through the forest instead of pebbles. His father left him and Gretel alone, just as he had done before, but this time the children were not worried. They went

cheerfully off to pick berries and gather dry sticks, and when they were
tired, they stopped for a rest.

When the sun set, Hansel began looking for the crumbs which would
show them the way home. But wherever he looked, and however hard
he peered at the ground, he could find nothing. The bread had gone.
The little birds had pecked up all the crumbs, and now Hansel and
Gretel were afraid. This time they really were lost in the depths of the
forest. They didn't know which way to go, so they simply followed their
noses and walked all night.

At last, as day was dawning, they came to a large clearing in the forest
and saw a little house standing on a small hill in the middle of it. It was
a wonderful little house, for the walls were made of gingerbread and the
roof was made of chocolate, and there were lollipops around the door
and window frames.

"I'll have a bit of the roof!" cried Hansel. "And you break off some of the
window frame, Gretel. It will taste nice and sweet!"

It did taste nice, too. The children hadn't eaten anything so delicious for
a very long time.

And as they broke off more pieces of the house and ate the delicious sweet stuff, they suddenly heard a quiet little voice:

Nibble, nibble, little mouse,
who's that nibbling at my house?

Hansel and Gretel looked at each other. Now they were caught!
"Our names are Hansel and Gretel," said Hansel, shyly. "We're lost, and we're dreadfully hungry."
As soon as he had said that the door opened, and out came a very ugly old woman.
"Don't be afraid, dear children," she said in a friendly voice. "Just come in and stay with me for a while, and I'll take good care of you."
However, the old woman was not really friendly, nor was she an ordinary old woman at all. She was a witch! Knowing that children love sweet things, she had made a house of gingerbread and chocolate, and when boys and girls came to nibble at her house, she lured them in – and ate them up herself. She took Hansel and Gretel by the hand, led them into her house and gave them all sorts of good things to eat: pancakes and apples and nuts. Finally they went to sleep in two pretty little white beds. Hansel and Gretel were very glad they had found this delicious house belonging to the nice old woman. It was much better than living with their cross stepmother at home.

When the witch saw the children asleep next morning, she felt a great longing to eat the tender meat from a child. However, she decided to wait a while, for she wanted to fatten them up first, particularly the little boy, or she would finish them up too soon.

She woke the children, seized Hansel, took him away and locked him up in a cage. Then she began fattening him up like a goose to make him round and plump, the way she liked children. Every day she brought him plates and bowls of food that looked wonderful and smelled delicious. She prepared the food herself, but Gretel had to help her with all the housework.

Poor Gretel was even worse off than Hansel. She had to work hard all day long, because the witch made her do all the unpleasant jobs she could think of, and Gretel had no delicious things to eat either, but always went hungry.

After about a week, the witch thought to herself that Hansel must be fat enough by now. She chuckled when she thought what a good meal the little boy would soon make her.

"Give me your hand, boy," she said, "so that I can feel it and see if you're nice and fat!"

However, Hansel was clever enough to stick a bone he had gnawed bare through the bars of his cage instead, and as the witch's eyesight was so

bad she thought it was his finger, and decided he was still too thin.

A day or so later she wanted to feel his finger again. Hansel gave her a bone to feel once more, and the old woman was surprised to find that he had not grown any fatter yet. She cooked more delicious food for him, and after a while she felt one of his fingers again. For the third time Hansel gave her a bone to feel, but this time the witch lost her temper. She was so hungry that she could wait no longer, and she said, "Gretel, go and fetch wood and light the oven. Whether he's fat or whether he's thin, I've waited long enough, and now I'm going to eat him."

Trembling with fear and terror, poor Gretel had to do as the witch asked, but she was trying hard to think of some way to save her brother.

When the fire in the stove began to crackle, the witch wanted to know if it was hot enough. So she opened the door and told Gretel to crawl into the oven and see if it was warming up. However, Gretel saw just what the witch was planning, and she said, "I don't know how to do that. How do I get into the oven?"

"You silly goose!" said the witch crossly. "It's easy! I'll show you!"

And she crouched down in front of the oven door and leaned forward.

That was just what Gretel was waiting for, and she gave the witch a mighty push. The witch fell right into the oven, and Gretel shut the door at once, so now they would have no more trouble with the wicked old woman.

Next Gretel went straight to Hansel's cage to set him free, and that wasn't easy, for by now he was so fat that he could hardly get out of the cage again.

The children wanted to escape as quickly as possible, but before they left they looked inside the witch's house once more, and that was just as well, for they found great baskets piled high with golden coins and sparkling jewels. The old woman must have been the wealthiest witch in the whole world!   They stuffed their pockets with gold and jewels, made bundles of their handkerchiefs, and Gretel put as much as she could carry into her apron.

"And now we must go!" said Hansel. "Let's see if we can find our way home again. Father must be very sad that we've been away so long."

So they set off. They took the first path they saw and walked for a long time, until they came to a river that barred their way.

"How can we get over this river?" asked Gretel in despair.

"Don't worry," said Hansel. "I'm sure we'll find some way to cross."

But although they tried hard, they could think of nothing, and the river never became narrow enough for them to jump over it, nor was there any bridge. They couldn't swim across because the current was too strong, and besides, all the jewels in their pockets weighed them down, and they would have sunk at once.

Then Gretel saw a beautiful white swan. "Dear swan," she asked, "can you help us over to the other side of this river?"

The swan said they could cross the river on its back. Gretel was afraid there would not be much room, but she sat on the swan's back and was carried safely over to the opposite bank. Hansel crossed after her. The children thanked the swan with all their hearts and went on their way again.

The forest grew thicker and thicker, but all of a sudden the children saw a path they knew. They must have been here before, and that meant they could not be far from home now. A little later they came to a small clearing in the forest, and then they saw their father's little house at last. Tired as they were, they ran in as fast as they could and hugged and kissed their father. He was so happy that he couldn't say a word at first; he just put one arm around Hansel and the other around Gretel, and danced through the room with them.

After a while he told them what had happened here at home. He still couldn't find enough wood to sell however hard he tried, and that made the children's stepmother so angry that she had packed and left. So their father had been alone all this time, alone and very sad, for he bitterly regretted leaving his children behind in the forest.

Hansel and Gretel told him all about their adventures, and at the end of their story they gave their father all the golden coins and jewels they had taken from the witch's house.

Now that the woodcutter had the witch's treasure, he did not need to work so hard, and the three of them lived happily together in their little house.

The Wishing Table

nce upon a time, very long ago, there was a poor tailor. He worked all day from early in the morning until late at night, yet he did not earn very much, for he had few customers, and those he did have weren't rich.

Indeed, the tailor earned so little that he couldn't buy his wife and his three sons anything to eat. Luckily he owned a goat, who gave plenty of milk, and when there was no money in the house the tailor and his family lived on nothing but milk and cheese. That usually happened a couple of times a week.

The goat was well cared for, of course. One of the tailor's three sons would take her out every day to pasture to graze. The goat hardly deserved such good treatment, for she had a cross, contrary nature, and would provoke people whenever she had the chance.

One morning the eldest son took her out to the churchyard where the juiciest, most tender grass grew. He let her run around there all day and choose whatever she wanted to eat.

When evening came, he asked the goat, "Dear, pretty goat, have you had enough to eat?"

And the goat nodded, her beard waving back and forth. "I've eaten so much I can't even jump over the hedge!" she said.

So the boy and the goat went back to the tailor's little house together. The boy put the goat in her shed, but as soon as he had gone away, she began to bleat.

She bleated so loud that the tailor came running at once. To his great surprise, the goat said, "I'm starving! Your son made me run all around the churchyard without getting a single blade of grass to eat." And the goat hung her head pitifully, as if she were quite worn out.

The tailor believed the goat, and was angry with his son. How could the boy be so cruel? Thanks to the goat, at least they always had milk and cheese in the house, and his son ought to have known better. He gave the goat a good feed of oats, which she thought delicious, and she ate it all up at once.

64

Leaving the goat, the tailor went to find his son. "How could you make that poor animal run around all day?" he said angrily. "Come here, and I'll teach you a lesson!" And he began beating his son with a stick.

"But I gave the goat plenty to eat!" said the poor boy. It was no use, however. His father just went on beating him, so the boy decided to run away from home.

He set off next morning, leaving the village without a word to anyone, and started out for the town. After a journey lasting several days he arrived, and to earn his living he apprenticed himself to a carpenter.

The boy was a handy lad, and his master was pleased with him. After a year he set out on his travels again, for he wanted to see more of the world. The carpenter thought it was a pity he was leaving, but he could understand why, for when he was young he had gone around the world himself. As a goodbye present, he gave the tailor's son a little table.

"It looks like any ordinary table, but it's worth a great deal," he told the boy. "Wherever you may be, it will conjure you up the most delicious things to eat by magic. All you have to do is say: Little table, lay yourself!"

The boy thanked the carpenter gratefully. He slung the little table on his back and set out, and when he had been walking for some time he stopped in the middle of a field.

"Little table, lay yourself!" he called.

Suddenly the table was covered with wonderful things to eat and drink: a big joint of meat, a cake, and a bottle of wine. The boy thought they looked delicious. He sat down at once and ate until he could eat no more, for the food tasted very good indeed.

When he had eaten his fill, the boy went on. He had a very easy journey, since he never needed to stay at an inn. He could sleep in a barn by night, and the little table made sure he had plenty to eat. It gave him different dishes every day, and he ate plenty of everything it provided.

After he had been on his travels for a few months he said to himself, "I think I'll go back to my father." It was a long time since he had last seen his family.

So next day he turned back to his father's house. He went along his way whistling happily, for he had thought of a good plan: he was going to give a party for the whole family and all their friends.

A good part of the journey was behind him by now, and if all went well he would be home next day. When evening came, he decided to sleep at an inn for once. The innkeeper showed him a room, and he shut the door, put down his little table and said, "Little table, lay yourself!" At once the table was covered with dishes of delicious food. Little did the boy know that the innkeeper was watching him through the keyhole. The man had felt curious when he heard the boy say, "Little table, lay yourself!", and now he saw all the delicious things to eat appear on the table. Hmm, thought the innkeeper, I'd like to get my hands on that little table. And that was what he did. In the night, while the boy was asleep, he

crept into his room and exchanged the little table for another that looked very like it. No one saw the innkeeper play this sly trick, for everyone else in the place was asleep, including the tailor's son.

Next day the boy, who had no idea what the innkeeper had done, went back to his father. He hugged the tailor and said, "Father, invite the whole family here. I'm going to give a party."

His father was very glad to see the boy back again, and he did indeed invite the whole family and all their friends. That evening the little house was full of guests.

"Little table, lay yourself!" cried the boy. But nothing happened, for this table couldn't make any food appear by magic, and the wishing table was hidden in the innkeeper's barn. Everyone laughed at the poor boy, and he felt very ashamed of himself.

The second son had trouble with the goat as well. One day he took her out to a wide pasture where she could graze on delicious grass all day long. In the evening the boy led her back to her shed, and a little later on the goat began to bleat. Along came the tailor and asked the goat what the matter was.

"I haven't had anything to eat today," bleated the goat, "and I've been made to run around all day long. I'm so tired I can hardly keep on my feet!"

The tailor flew into a rage and went for his son with a stick. Whatever the second son said, his father wouldn't stop beating him, so the second son ran away too.

He went to work for a miller, and stayed with him for a year. Then he decided to go home again. The miller, who was very pleased with the boy's work, said, "My lad, I'm going to give you a present. Go to the stable and lead out the donkey you'll find there. He is able to do something no other donkey can, and it's a trick you'll find very handy."

The boy led out the donkey, thinking to himself: this isn't much of a present! That donkey is a lazy beast and never does any work. He just stands in the stable daydreaming.

However, the boy was wrong. "Spit it out, little donkey!" said the miller, and the animal immediately began spitting golden coins.

That same day the boy set off for his father's house, and he stopped for the night at the inn where his brother had stayed before him. The curious innkeeper wondered why the boy shut himself up alone with his donkey in the room. Once again, he looked through the keyhole, and he discovered the secret of the golden coins. On the sly, he exchanged the donkey for an animal that looked just like it, and he put the donkey who could spit golden coins in a safe place in his own stable.

When the second son came home next day, he promised his father a great heap of money.

"Spit it out, little donkey!" he cried, but nothing happened.

The tailor thought to himself: my two eldest sons have lost their wits! A little table that conjures up food by magic, a donkey who spits out golden coins ... whoever heard such nonsense?

"I am going to learn the woodcutter's trade," said the tailor's youngest son to his two elder brothers one day. "I'm tired of being beaten all the time because the goat says I don't give her enough to eat."

"Then mind you remember one thing," said his eldest brother. "When you come back again, watch out for the innkeeper who stole our treasures."

Next day the third son left home. He worked for a woodcutter for a year, and because he worked hard his master was very pleased with him. At the end of the year, the tailor's third son wanted to go home too.

"I have a present for you," said his master, and he brought out a linen bag. "There's a cudgel in this bag. When you want it to hit someone, just call: Out of the bag, cudgel! And when you want it to stop, just call: Into the bag, cudgel! and the cudgel will do whatever you say." So the woodcutter gave the boy the bag with the cudgel in it.

The youngest son set off for home, and on the way he met two thieves who tried to steal his money.

"Out of the bag, cudgel!" he called. The bag immediately opened, and out came the cudgel. It began dealing the thieves mighty blows, and the boy didn't have to do anything to defend himself. "Into the bag, cudgel!" he said when the thieves had run away, and the cudgel did just as he asked.

After a few days on the road the boy came to the inn where his two brothers had stayed.

"I have nothing special in this bag of mine!" he said, loud enough for the innkeeper to hear him. And he stayed awake on watch that night, wondering whether the innkeeper would try to steal his bag.

That was exactly what happened. In the middle of the night the innkeeper crept into the boy's room, picked up the bag. and was about to make off with it. But the boy called, "Out of the bag, cudgel! Beat that thief until he gives back what he stole!"

Crash, bang, wham! How that cudgel did beat the innkeeper! The man ran straight to his barn and fetched the donkey and the little table.

"I'll never do anything bad again!" he wailed. "Have mercy – make the cudgel stop beating me, please do! Ouch, my poor back!"

Next day, early in the afternoon, the tailor's youngest son arrived home.

"Father, invite all our family to a party!" said he. The tailor feared something would go wrong again, but he did as his son asked, and that evening the little house was full of guests once more.

The middle brother led his donkey into the middle of the room and cried, "Spit it out, little donkey!" Immediately gold coins rolled out of the donkey's mouth.

Then the eldest brother put his little table down and said, "Little table, lay yourself!" and great dishes full of the most delicious food you can imagine appeared on the table.

The guests were delighted. Each of them got a handful of golden coins, and enough to eat for a whole week. It was a wonderful party, and the tailor was very proud of his three sons.

And for the rest of his life, the old tailor never had to use his needle again, for he had plenty of money. Whenever he wanted golden coins he could get them from the little donkey.

His wife didn't have to work hard either, for she never had to cook now.
But she did roast a joint of meat herself once more – the very next day,
when the family had goat for their dinner, for they were sick and tired of
the animal's tricks.

The Wolf and the Seven Little Kids

nce upon a time Mother Goat lived with her seven little kids in a small but very comfortable house on the outskirts of the forest. She loved her children dearly, for they were the nicest, prettiest little kids in the whole world. They played games with one another all day long: hide and seek, and tag, and leapfrog. And they were

never bored, because there was always a little brother or sister who felt like a game too.

Mother Goat wanted her children to grow up to be strong, big, healthy goats. And if a kid is to grow up big and strong, it must eat good, nourishing food and go to bed early, just like a human child. However, it wasn't always easy for Mother Goat to give all her children enough to eat, because they were hungry the whole time. No sooner did she get fresh greenstuff into the house than one of those hungry kids would be munching it.

One day everything eatable in the house had disappeared into their little stomachs. So Mother Goat called all her children together and said, "Now listen to me, and listen carefully, because I'm going to tell you something very important."

She stopped, looked at the faces of all her seven children to make sure they were listening properly, and then went on. "I'm going into the woods to look for nice food for you – "

"Goody, goody!" cried a kid called Skippy. "Just what I want! I've been feeling I could do with something nice to eat all morning. Good idea, Mother!"

"Let your mother finish what she's saying, you greedy little thing!" said Mother Goat. "Now listen: when I'm not here to look after you, you must look after yourselves. You're quite big enough to do that now. But above all, watch out for the wolf, for if he comes along you're in great danger. So keep the door locked, don't go outside to play, and don't open the door to anyone. Do you understand all that?"

"Why is the wolf dangerous, Mother?" asked a kid called Hoppy, who always wanted to know reasons for everything.

"Because wolves think kids are good to eat," replied Mother Goat. "And since wolves are often hungry, they go prowling around looking for good things to eat. Wolves think kids make a delicious meal, so that's why they're dangerous. Now, will you be careful to do as I say?"

"Yes, Mother," said the seven little kids in chorus.

So Mother Goat kissed her children and went out to look for nice juicy greens for them to eat.

Meanwhile all the little kids went indoors to play a game. They hadn't been playing for ten minutes when … what was that? The sound of someone knocking at the door! The kids looked at one another. They were going to open the door, but they remembered what their mother had said just in time. Could this be the wolf?

Yes, it really was the wolf! He had been hiding behind a tree when

Mother Goat went out to look for nice things to eat. Aha, thought the wolf, now those silly little kids are all alone! I could just do with a few tender morsels to eat, and little kids are more tender and delicious than anything else!

So the wolf made a wicked plan, for of course he knew Mother Goat must have told her children to be careful and watch out for him.

When the door wasn't opened at once, the wolf knocked again, and the bravest of the kids, Patch, asked in a trembling voice, "Who's there?"

"Why, dear children, it's me back again!" said a voice on the other side of the door. "I've brought you some lovely things to eat, so just open the door at once, will you?"

However, even the smallest kid of all, called Wagtail, could tell at once that it wasn't their mother standing at the door. Their mother's voice was quite different, and besides, she hadn't been gone long. She could never have found enough food for all her seven little kids so quickly!

"We won't open the door," called the little kids in chorus. "Our mother's voice is much softer and sweeter than yours! We think you're the wicked wolf and you want to eat us up."

The wolf was baffled. He had never thought the kids might guess he wasn't their mother from the sound of his voice. These tender morsels were cleverer than he had expected! He didn't try getting into the house again, but went back into the forest instead.

He knew there was a beehive in the forest, under an old lime tree. The bees were not friends of his, for he often tormented them, but he had to go to their hive if he wanted some honey. He was stung on his nose and his forepaws, but he managed to steal a big honeycomb and ate it up at once. Honey is very good for the voice, and the best honey is so sweet that it will even sweeten your voice.

When the wolf tried his voice out, it didn't sound as rough as before. "They'll believe me this time," he muttered, and he laughed a nasty laugh.

He went back to the little house and tried again. "There now, dear children, here's your mother back again. Oh, what good things I've brought you home!"

Inside the house, the little kids looked at one another. Could it really be their mother this time? The voice sounded softer and sweeter, but the little kids were not sure. This couldn't be the wolf, whose voice was quite different, but was it Mother Goat herself?

One of the kids had an idea. He lay flat on the floor and looked under the door.

"No," he said, "that's not Mother. Mother has white feet, and whoever's out there has brown paws. It's the wolf trying his tricks on us again."

"It's the wolf, it's the wolf!" shouted all the kids at once. "And Mother says we mustn't let you in!"

Growling furiously, the wolf went away again. Those kids were not only wonderfully tender but wonderfully clever too. Perhaps that was what made them so delicious! But just wait, he'd show them! He went to the mill as fast as he could go, hid behind a woodpile and peered around it to see if the miller was in sight, but he saw no one.

Fast as an arrow from the bow he shot into the mill. The miller was high up at the top of the mill, working with the man who helped him. The wolf could hear their voices.

There was a big crate of nice, finely ground white flour standing there, and the wolf jumped straight in and then straight out again. He moved so fast that the miller and his man never noticed him at all.

Now the wolf's paws were white as snow, and he ran back to the little house with the kids inside. He knocked on the door and called, "Well, children, here's your mother back. You can open the door now!"

"Let's see your feet first," the little kids called back, "because the wicked wolf has been here twice, but we didn't let him in."

"Very sensible of you, children," said the wolf, still speaking in a soft, friendly voice, as if he were Mother Goat. "But take a good look at my feet. They're as white as ever."

The little kids all looked under the door one by one, and they saw their mother's white feet. Yes, it must be safe to open the door now! So they unlocked the door as fast as they could, and immediately they discovered their mistake!

They scattered in all directions, trying to hide under the table and in the cupboard, in their mother's bed and behind her rocking chair. The youngest, Wagtail, disappeared into the big grandfather clock. He quickly opened the door, hid inside and closed the door again – just in time, for the wolf had reached the living room now.

The wolf tracked the poor little kids down quite easily, one by one, and he ate them all up in great gulps. He was so hungry that he didn't even chew properly; he just swallowed the kids hide and hair and all.

When he had eaten six kids and he couldn't see any more, he thought he must have found them all. He had eaten quite enough anyway – indeed, more than enough!

So the wolf dragged himself and his great swollen stomach outside, lay down under the first tree he came to and fell asleep at once. What a lovely meal it had been! His belly was as fat as a football, and even in his sleep the wolf dreamed of delicious, tender little kids.

Then Mother Goat came home and had a dreadful fright. The door was wide open, and the whole house had been turned upside down. Chairs,

tables and cupboards were all knocked over, and her children had disappeared!

She went to the attic and called out the names of her seven children one after another: "Hoppy, Skippy, Patch!"

There was no answer. Sad and frightened, she came downstairs and called again. And then ... then she heard a noise somewhere. But where did it come from? She called once more, and once again there was an answer. "I'm inside the clock, Mother!" said Wagtail. "But I can't open the door from this side."

Mother Goat quickly opened the door of the clock and set her youngest child free. The kid was trembling like a leaf, huddled in the furthest corner of the clock case with great tears of fright in his eyes. Sobbing, Wagtail told Mother Goat what had happened: how the wolf had come knocking at the door, but they didn't open it until he came back for the third time with his paws as white as a goat's feet, and then he came in and ate all her children.

"Except for me, because he couldn't find me," said Wagtail, and he began shaking all over again when he thought of the wolf.

78

"Yes, what luck, except for you! At least I still have you," wept Mother Goat. "But oh, my six dear children!"

They went outside together, and suddenly they heard the wolf snoring. Keeping close together, they followed the sound. And there lay the wolf, still fast asleep after his good meal.

His stomach was so fat and swollen that when Mother Goat saw him lying there tears came to her eyes. It was her dear little children making him so fat. She looked at the wolf so long and so hard that she suddenly thought she saw something moving inside his belly. Surely she was wrong, and it must be the tears blurring her sight! So she blinked, and wiped the tears away, and she still saw something moving. It wasn't her tears after all. The wolf's belly really was twitching.

"Quick," she told Wagtail, "run home and fetch me a knife and a needle and thread. Run as fast as you possibly can, and perhaps we can still save your little brothers and sisters."

The little kid ran off as fast as his hooves would carry him, and came back very soon with a knife, a needle and thread.

Then Mother Goat slit the wolf's belly open. He was so fast asleep that he didn't even wake up. One by one the six little kids jumped out, safe and sound – the wolf was so greedy that he had swallowed them whole. Mother Goat gave all her children a kiss, and hugged them each in turn. But there was still work to be done. "Quick, children," she said. "Find me some rocks about the same size and the same weight as yourselves, and roll them over here."

The kids found rocks so big they couldn't carry them, and had to roll them over to their mother using their heads and their hooves. Then Mother Goat stuffed the wolf's belly with the rocks and sewed it up with big stitches. She had soon finished, and the goats all ran home as fast as they could go, went inside the house and closed the door. They went to stand at the windows and see what happened next.

No sooner were they indoors than the wolf woke up. "Oh, what a pain I have in my stomach!" he groaned. "And how thirsty I am! I must have eaten too much. I ought to have kept a few of those kids for later. Oh, my poor tummy!"

The wolf rose to his feet with difficulty, and dragged his heavy body over to the stream to drink. A nice drink of cool water would make him feel better, he thought.

The rocks in his belly rumbled against each other as he moved, and when he finally reached the stream he was hardly able to keep on his feet. He put his head down to the water to drink, but then all the rocks inside him rolled forward, so that he fell straight into the stream. It happened to be very deep just there, and however hard the wolf tried to swim, the heavy rocks in his belly dragged him down to the bottom.

From then on Mother Goat and her children never had to fear the wolf, and later, when the kids grew up and had children themselves, they often told the exciting story of the Wolf and the Seven Little Kids.

Snow White and the Seven Dwarfs

It was midwinter, and snowflakes were swirling through the air like feathers. The queen sat doing her embroidery at the window in a beautiful room in the palace. It was pleasantly warm in the room, for a fire was burning in the hearth, and the queen looked around her. What a fine room it was, with all its handsome furniture, and the beautiful wooden frame of the window, which was made of dark ebony, almost black. From time to time the queen looked out at the snow, and that made her careless, so that she pricked her finger and three drops of blood fell on the snow lying on the window sill. The red blood looked so pretty against the white of the snow and the black of the ebony that the queen thought: oh, if only I could have a child as white as snow, as red as blood and as black as ebony!

The queen had not been married to the king for very long, and had only just come to live in the castle. Although of course she was very happy with the king, she longed for a child. She thought a little baby, best of all a daughter, would be the nicest thing in the world.

Quite soon her wish came true. She had a little daughter with hair as black as ebony, skin as pale as snow, and lips as red as blood. The queen remembered the day she sat by the window doing her embroidery, and she called the little girl Snow White. However, when the baby had been born the queen her mother died.

A year later the king married a new wife. She was beautiful, but proud and vain, and she wanted to be mistress over everyone. She thought she was the most beautiful woman in the whole world, and felt sure no one could be nearly as lovely as herself. The mere idea that a girl just as beautiful as she was might be born some day sent her into a rage.

Now the new queen had a magic mirror, and whenever she sat admiring herself in the mirror she would ask it:

Mirror, mirror on the wall,
who is fairest of us all?

And the mirror replied:

Queen, you are loveliest of all!

Then the queen was satisfied, for she knew the mirror always told the truth. She would stay sitting in front of the mirror for a while, brushing her hair and admiring herself in her fine clothes.
Meanwhile, Snow White was growing up and becoming prettier every day. When she was seven she was a lovely little girl, and you could tell she would be much more beautiful than the queen had ever been. Indeed, she was lovelier than her stepmother already!
One day, when the queen asked her mirror again:

Mirror, mirror on the wall,
who is fairest of us all?

the mirror gave her an answer she had not expected:

Oh queen, though beautiful you are
Snow White is lovelier by far!

The queen was furious, and turned green and yellow with rage. She had been jealous of Snow White from the first moment she set eyes on the little girl. But from now on she hated her stepdaughter – the child who dared to be lovelier than herself, the queen of the land!
Matters grew worse as the queen became more and more jealous. Every day she saw how much the king loved his daughter, and she knew that all the servants in the palace loved the child dearly too. Snow White seemed to be growing more beautiful daily. The queen had jars full of ointments to put on her face, but they did no good: she was getting less beautiful, while Snow White became lovelier all the time.
In the end she could bear it no longer. She summoned one of the huntsmen and told him, "Take the child away! I never want to set eyes on her again! You must kill her, and bring me back her liver and heart as proof that you have carried out my orders."
The huntsman said he understood, and he took Snow White deep into the forest with him. The little girl liked it there, and she danced and played happily around the huntsman. The birds sang their sweetest

songs, and the rabbits and deer let her stroke them. But when the huntsman brought out his knife to do as the queen had ordered him and kill the girl, she began to cry, and begged the man to spare her life. "I will hide deep in this forest and never come back to the palace again," she promised, sobbing.

She was so pretty and so sweet that the huntsman felt sorry for her and said, "Run away quickly then, poor child. I'll say I've killed you, and I'm sure the queen will believe me."

He thought the wild animals would soon attack her and tear her to pieces, so then she would be dead anyway, and the idea made him sad, yet he felt a weight lift from his heart to think he did not have to kill Snow White himself.

Seeing a roe deer among the trees close to him, he shot the animal and took its heart and liver back to the queen, pretending they were Snow White's.

Left alone in the forest, Snow White was dreadfully frightened. It was so quiet, except for the rustling all around. Was that the sound of animals running away from her ... or were the wild beasts about to attack her?

She began to run faster and faster in her fear of the strange noises and of her wicked stepmother, who had wanted her killed. Perhaps the queen had sent another servant after her to make sure she was really dead!

It was evening when she suddenly saw a little house. By now Snow White was very tired, and her clothes were torn from the prickly bushes she had passed. She couldn't understand it: how could there be a little house here in the middle of such a great, wild forest? And who could live there?

The door of the house was not locked. Snow White knocked, and called softly, "Is there anyone there? May I come in?" When no one appeared, and there was no answer, she went inside. She was very tired, and wanted to rest.

All was neat and tidy inside the house. There was a table with seven little chairs around it, laid with seven plates, seven mugs, seven forks and seven spoons on a fine white tablecloth. Seven beds stood in a long row against the whitewashed wall, each with a pretty blanket on it.

But how small it all was! Snow White thought it looked like a house for

dolls. However, she did not stop to wonder any more, for she was very tired and very hungry, and there was bread on the plates, while the mugs were full of milk.

Although she was so hungry, she did not want to eat everything off a single plate, so she took a little bit of bread from each of the seven plates, and drank a sip of milk from each little mug. You could hardly see that anything had gone.

Then, because she was so tired, she went to lie down on one of the little beds. She tried them all, but most of them were much too short for her. Finally she came to the seventh bed, and it fitted her exactly. She pulled the blanket over her, and immediately fell fast asleep.

When it was quite dark the owners of the little house came home. They were seven dwarfs who worked in the mountains, mining ore from early in the morning until late at night. They went out every morning singing happily, and every evening they came home to their little house in the forest singing happily too.

Once they were home, the dwarfs lit a lamp, and they immediately saw that someone had been in their house.

"Who's been sitting in my chair?" asked the first.

"Who's been eating from my plate?" asked the second.

The third wondered who had been nibbling at his bread, and the fourth thought someone had been drinking his milk.

The fifth said someone had used his fork.

"And who's been cutting with my knife?" asked the sixth dwarf.

The seventh pointed to his bed, and said, "Someone's been sleeping in my bed."

The others looked at their own beds, and one after another they saw that their beds didn't look just as they had left them that morning.

Then they suddenly fell silent, for they had all seen Snow White at the same moment. There she lay, peacefully asleep. Eyes wide with surprise, holding their breath, they looked at the sleeping girl.

"How beautiful she is!" sighed one of them, and the others agreed. They had never seen such a lovely girl before.

They decided not to wake her, but ate their supper and drank their milk, keeping very quiet so that Snow White could sleep. After supper they went to bed themselves, and two of the dwarfs shared a bed, because Snow White was still asleep in the seventh bed.

When it was almost morning Snow White woke up, and she was afraid when she saw the seven dwarfs standing around her bed, looking at her. Fortunately they were very friendly, and asked her name, and where she came from, and how she had found their little house.

So she told them how her stepmother had wanted the huntsman to kill her, but he had spared her life, and she had walked all day until she found the house where the dwarfs lived.

"Will you keep house for us?" the dwarfs asked Snow White. "Will you do the cooking, make the beds, sew and knit and keep everything neat and clean? If so, you are welcome to stay with us, and you will have everything you need."

"Oh, yes," said Snow White. "I would like that very much!" So she stayed with the dwarfs and kept house for them.

Every morning the dwarfs went to the mountains to mine copper and gold, and every evening, when they came home, they wanted their supper to be ready. Snow White was left alone all day, but she didn't mind that. She had plenty to do, and besides, she liked watching the birds and the forest animals.

However, the dwarfs warned her, "Beware of your stepmother. She will

soon find out that the huntsman didn't kill you and you're here, so don't open the door to anyone. Will you remember that?"

Sure enough, the wicked queen did find out what had happened. When she saw the heart and liver the huntsman brought her she thought that now she would be the fairest of all again, just as she was before Snow White became so beautiful. However, of course she wanted to hear it and be sure, so she went to look in her mirror and asked:

Mirror, mirror on the wall,
who is fairest of us all?

And the mirror replied:

Oh queen, though beautiful you are
over the mountains far away
Snow White lives with the dwarfs today,
and she is lovelier by far!

The queen went white with rage, for she knew the mirror could not lie, and she realized that the huntsman had cheated her and Snow White was still alive.

She immediately began to think of new ways to kill Snow White. Whatever happened, she, the queen, must be the fairest lady in the land again, so she must get rid of the girl. She soon thought of a plan: she dyed her hair and disguised herself as an old pedlar woman, so that no one could guess she was the queen.

In this disguise, the queen crossed the mountains to the seven dwarfs' house. When she saw it in the distance, she began to call, "Fine wares for sale! Fine wares for sale!"

Snow White looked out of the window to see who was crying her wares, and when the queen came closer she asked, "What do you have for sale?"

"Fine things, pretty things!" said the woman. "Pretty ribbons and belts and laces!" And she showed Snow White a pretty belt of woven silk.

Surely I can let this good old woman in, thought the girl, opening the door to the pedlar. She bought the beautiful belt, and the woman said she would fasten it neatly around her waist. "For you are a little untidy," said the old woman, "and this will make you look better."

Snow White agreed, and went to stand in front of the woman so that she could fasten the belt around her waist. However, the wicked queen put the belt around her so quickly and pulled it so tight that Snow White could not draw breath, and she fell to the ground unconscious. She seemed to have stopped breathing, and her face went pale as death.

"Now I am the loveliest in the land again," murmured the pedlar woman, with an evil laugh, and she quickly went away.

Not long after this the seven dwarfs came home, and they were horrified to see their dear little friend lying unconscious on the floor. Seeing that her belt was pulled much too tight, they cut it at once. The girl began to breathe again and a little pink came back into her face. When the dwarfs heard what had happened, they said the old pedlar woman could only have been the wicked queen.

"From now on you must remember not to let anyone in when we are not at home," they said. "We told you so before, and you know that your stepmother is a very wicked woman."

Once the queen was home again she went straight to her magic mirror and asked:

Mirror, mirror on the wall,
who is fairest of us all?

And the mirror replied, just as it always did:

Oh queen, though beautiful you are
over the mountains far away
Snow White lives with the dwarfs today,
and she is lovelier by far!

When she heard that, the queen thought she would fall down in a faint, she was so furious to hear that Snow White was still alive. I must and will think of some way to be rid of that creature for good, she thought. Now the queen could work magic, and so she made a poisoned comb. Then she disguised herself as an old woman again, but a different old woman this time.

Once again she crossed the mountains, came to the little house where the seven dwarfs lived, knocked on the door and cried, "Fine wares for sale! Good wares for sale!"

Snow White looked out of the window and said, "Go away! I mustn't let anyone in."

"You can just look, I suppose?" said the old woman, and she took out the poisoned comb and held it up.

The girl thought the comb so pretty that she let the old woman talk her into opening the door. Then the pedlar said, "Your hair is very untidy, my child. Let me comb it for you."

Poor Snow White, never guessing that this might be her wicked stepmother, let the old woman have her way, but as soon as the comb touched her hair the poison began to work, and she fell lifeless to the floor.

"There, my beauty!" said the old woman, laughing maliciously. "That's the end of you!" And she hurried away and soon disappeared into the forest.

Luckily the dwarfs came home not long after she had gone.

When they saw Snow White lying on the floor once more, they immediately thought of her stepmother, and searched until they found the poisoned comb.

As soon as they had taken it out of the girl's hair she began to breathe again, a little pink came back into her cheeks, and she told them what had happened. Yet again the dwarfs warned her to be very, very careful, and above all not to open the door to anyone.

Once the queen was home, she looked in her mirror and asked:

Mirror, mirror on the wall,
who is fairest of us all?

And the mirror replied, just as it always did:

> *Oh queen, though beautiful you are*
> *over the mountains far away*
> *Snow White lives with the dwarfs today,*
> *and she is lovelier by far!*

When the queen heard that she began to shake all over with rage. "Snow White must die!" she cried. "She must die if it costs me my own life!"

She went to a secret room where no one but herself was ever allowed, and there she made a poisoned apple. It was pretty to look at, bright red, so that it looked very good to eat, but anyone who took a bite of it would be sure to die!

When the apple was ready the queen stained her face and disguised herself as an old peasant woman. She crossed the mountains to the house where the dwarfs lived again, and knocked on the door. Snow White put her head out of the window and said, "I mustn't let anyone in. The seven dwarfs have forbidden me to open the door."

"Oh, never mind that," said the farmer's wife. "I want to get rid of my apples – here, you can have one for nothing."

"Oh no," said Snow White, "I mustn't take any presents either."

"Are you afraid of poison?" asked the woman. "Look, I'll cut the apple in half. You can eat the red side and I'll eat the other half. Then we'll both be eating the same apple, and you can be sure there's nothing wrong with it."

But the apple was so cunningly made that only the red side was poisoned. Snow White longed to eat it, and when she saw the farmer's wife bite into the apple herself she couldn't resist putting out her hand to take the poisoned half.

No sooner did she take a bit of the apple into her mouth than she fell to the floor dead. The queen gave her a look full of malice, laughed aloud and said, "White as snow, red as blood and black as ebony – but this time the dwarfs will never be able to bring you back to life."

As soon as she came home, she asked her mirror:

> *Mirror, mirror on the wall,*
> *who is fairest of us all?*

And at long last the mirror replied:

> *Queen, you are loveliest of all!*

Now her magic had worked, she was the loveliest in the land again, and Snow White would not disturb her peace any more!

When the dwarfs came home that evening they found Snow White lying on the floor. She lay perfectly still, she was not breathing, and her face was even paler than last time. Her eyes were closed. This time she was really dead.

They picked her up and looked to see if they could find any trace of poison. They loosened her dress, combed her hair and washed her with water and with wine, but nothing did any good. Their dear little friend was dead and gone.

They laid her on a bed, and all seven of them sat around it and wept and wailed for three days. Then they were going to bury her, but she still looked as if she were alive. Her hair shone, her lips were still as red as blood, and she was so lovely that they said, "We can't bury her in the dark earth where no one will see how sweet and beautiful she is."

They had a glass coffin made, so that she could be seen from all sides, laid her in it and wrote her name on the coffin in gold letters, saying that she was a king's daughter. They put the coffin at the foot of the mountains, and one of them always stayed by it to watch over it.

The birds came and mourned for Snow White too: first came an owl, then a raven, and last of all a dove. And the deer came as well, and the rabbits, and all the other animals whom Snow White had loved. Snow White lay in her glass coffin for a long, long time, and she always looked as if she were only sleeping.

One day a prince was riding through the forest. He came to the little house where the dwarfs lived, and as it was late and would soon be quite dark, he asked if he could spend the night with them. Then he saw the coffin, with the beautiful girl inside who looked as if she were asleep.

The prince had never seen such a sweet and lovely girl before, and he knew he would always love her. He read the golden letters written on the glass coffin, and begged the dwarfs to let him take it and the girl away with him. "You can have whatever you like in return," said he, "but give her to me! She is so lovely and so sweet that I want her with me always. I will take the greatest care of her, and I promise you there will always be a soldier on guard by the glass coffin."

But the dwarfs would not let Snow White go, whatever the prince offered them.

He persisted, however, saying, "If I may take her with me I will guard her as my most precious treasure. I cannot live without her, even if I can only look at her."

When he said this the dwarfs felt sorry for him, and they agreed to let him take Snow White away in her coffin.

The prince told his servants to carry the coffin on their shoulders.

However, one of the men stumbled, and the coffin fell to the ground with Snow White inside it. It struck the ground with a crack, broke into a dozen pieces, and everyone cried out in alarm.

Then something quite unexpected happened. The shock jolted the piece of apple out of Snow White's throat, and she opened her eyes, sat up, and looked around her in surprise.

"Good gracious, where am I?" she asked.

The prince said, in great delight, "You are with me!" He told her what had happened, and said, "I love you more than anything else in the world. Will you go to my father's castle with me, marry me and be my queen?"

Snow White was glad to agree, for she saw at once that the prince was a good, kind young man. She said goodbye to the dwarfs, and went to the prince's own country with him.

There were great festivities at their wedding, to which a great many guests were invited, including Snow White's wicked stepmother. She thought it would be pleasant to go to the wedding, although of course she did not know the bride was Snow White. When she had put on her finest dress she went to her magic mirror and asked:

Mirror, mirror on the wall,
who is fairest of us all?

And the mirror replied:

Oh queen, though beautiful you are,
the bride is lovelier by far!

Then the queen fell into such a rage as she had never felt before. She went into her magic room and locked the door, so that no one could get her out again. After a while the palace servants had to break the door down, but they found the room empty. The door had been locked all the time, all the windows were closed, yet the wicked queen had disappeared, and nothing more was ever heard of her.

After their magnificent wedding Snow White and her prince lived happily together for many years, and every week all seven dwarfs came visiting to play with Snow White's children, who were all as sweet and pretty as their mother.

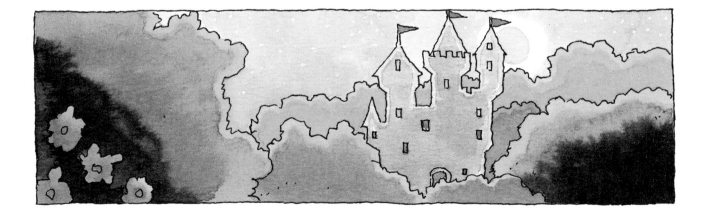

One Eye, Two Eyes, and Three Eyes

Once upon a time three sisters lived in a country far away. The eldest had only one eye, the youngest had three eyes, and the middle sister had two eyes like anyone else. However, they none of them knew that most people had two eyes, so Two Eyes was teased by her two sisters and even her mother, who all thought her a strange kind of child, with her silly two eyes. Only did they tease her, they made her do all the hard housework and wear ragged clothes, and if she didn't obey their orders at once they would beat her. She was given nothing to eat all day, and only in the evening, when her mother and sisters had eaten a delicious meal, would they throw her the bones to gnaw. The poor child was not used to any better treatment, so she didn't complain, but did her work every day and never said a word of all she suffered at home.

This could not go on for ever, and one day Two Eyes could not bear it any more and ran away from her work, closing the door of the house behind her. She went out to the meadow where her pet goat was grazing, intending to weep her heart out with her face buried in the goat's soft fleece.

So she sat down in the grass and burst out sobbing. The goat was alarmed, and moved a little way off. She began eating grass, and looked at Two Eyes as if to say, "What's the matter? What good does this weeping and wailing do you? I don't want such a noise in my meadow!" But suddenly the goat stopped gazing at Two Eyes and looked the other way, her eyes wide with surprise. For there was a great rose growing in the meadow, where no rose had grown before, and what was more, in the middle of the rose stood a fairy.

The fairy was a beautiful sight, and she was looking kindly at Two Eyes, who still sat in the grass, sobbing.

"Why are you so sad?" she asked.

"My sister and my mothers torment me so!" said Two Eyes. "And I'm hungry, dreadfully hungry, because I haven't had anything to eat since yesterday, and I didn't get much yesterday evening either, nothing but some water warmed up in a greasy pan which had held a delicious dish for my mother and my sisters."

And Two Eyes began to cry again even harder, and told the fairy she was always cold, because she had nothing to wear but her two sisters' cast-offs, which they gave her when they didn't want them any more. So she had only thin, ragged clothes, even in winter.

"Hush now, Two Eyes, and listen to me," said the fairy in gentle tones. "I will make your goat able to help you. You have only to remember the few words I tell you, and whenever you say them to the goat you can have as much as you like to eat. Listen, for you must remember them:

Little goat, bleat,
bring me food to eat.

And when you have had enough, you must say:

Little goat, I say,
take the food away.

There, that's not so difficult, is it? I am sure you can remember it. So sit down and eat your fill."
As soon as she had said these words, the fairy vanished as suddenly as she had come.
Two Eyes immediately did as the fairy had told her, and said, "Little goat, bleat! Bring me food to eat." No sooner had she spoken the words than she saw a table standing before her, laden with all kinds of delicious things. Two Eyes tried all the dishes, ate some of the candied fruits, took a few spoonfuls of jam and honey, and sank her teeth into a bright red apple. When she had eaten all she could she said, "Little goat, I say! Take the food away." And a moment later there was nothing to be seen.
Two Eyes stared at her goat.
Who would have thought a goat could provide such nice things to eat? And the goat looked back at Two Eyes, as if to say, "I'd never have thought I could work magic either, although of course I always knew I was a very special goat."
When evening came, Two Eyes went home. Obedient as ever, she did

everything her mother and sisters told her to do, but she didn't touch the few scraps of food they gave her.

Next day she went out to the meadow again with her goat, and at noon she made the little table appear once more. She sat down and enjoyed all the good things on the little table, and then made it disappear again. After that she lay down to sleep, comfortably full of food.

Several days passed, and no one noticed anything unusual. Her mother and sisters took so little notice of Two Eyes that they hadn't even realized she was looking better than usual, while she left the food they gave her alone.

However, after a week One Eye and Three Eyes did begin to suspect something. Two Eyes had never looked so well, yet they were giving her no more to eat than usual. What could the explanation be? They had to know more, and they were determined to find out their sister's secret. They soon made a plan.

Next day, they decided, One Eye would go out with Two Eyes to the goat in the meadow, for they guessed that what-ever was going on must happen there. If Two Eyes had hidden anything in the house, they would

have found it long ago. Pretending to smile, One Eye told Two Eyes that she would like to go out to the meadow with her, and they would be company for each other.

Two Eyes knew just why her sister was suddenly taking such an interest in her. One Eye was planning something bad. However, Two Eyes said nothing, and made a plan of her own to be rid of her sister.

Next morning, as usual, Two Eyes got up while the cockerel himself was still asleep. Even the sun had not yet risen. Two Eyes had all kinds of household tasks to do before she could go out to the meadow, and when they were finished she woke One Eye to go with her.

This time she chose a path leading to a place where the grass was particu-larly green and tender. The goat would have good grazing there. But it was a long walk, and One Eye, who never exerted herself much, soon felt very tired, while her sister hopped and skipped along the path. At last One Eye lay down in a hollow in the ground and fell asleep. Two Eyes took her chance, and said at once, "Little goat, bleat! Bring me food to eat!" And after eating a good meal she made the little table disappear again, as usual. When One Eye woke, there was nothing to be seen. Once

home, she noticed that Two Eyes left her dish of scraps untouched again, but still she didn't know why Two Eyes no longer gnawed the leftover bones to get every scrap of meat off them, as she used to.

As soon as Two Eyes had gone to her attic to sleep, the other three put their heads together. They must and would find out her secret! They decided that Three Eyes would go out to the meadow with Two Eyes next day.

Once again Two Eyes chose a place where tall grass grew, some way from the house. In her own turn, Three Eyes became very tired. She stretched out at the foot of a tree and immediately fell asleep. But although it looked as if her middle eye were closed, like the other two, it wasn't. She was only pretending, meaning to trick Two Eyes.

Two Eyes did not see that her sister's extra, cunning eye was still awake, and she made the little table appear, ate a delicious meal, and then made the table disappear once more. Her sister peeped through the lashes of her third eye and saw it all. That evening she told her mother and One Eye the whole story.

"What a little wretch!" cried their mother. "What an ungrateful child! Didn't she stop to think we might enjoy the delicious food from her table too? She might have asked us if we'd like to share her meal! As for the goat, I suppose it's a magic goat, and that can do us no good, for you can't trust magic animals. A goat like that is dangerous." And in a fury, the mother snatched up a knife, went out to the meadow where the goat was grazing, and stabbed the poor creature to death.

Next day, when Two Eyes heard what had happened, she ran out of the house to hide her grief.

She knew she was going to weep bitterly for her poor goat, and she didn't want her mother and her sisters to see her.

Heartbroken, she was sitting in the grass, sobbing, when the fairy suddenly appeared again and asked her what the matter was.

"Oh, dear fairy," wept the girl, "my sister Three Eyes found out the secret of my goat, and my mother killed it. How am I ever to get enough to eat now? My mother will eat the meat of the goat herself – my poor dear goat, who always brought me my little table by magic."

The fairy thought about it, wrinkling her forehead, and then she had an idea.

"Ask for the goat's left front hoof, and bury it outside the house," she said. "Then you will live a long and happy life."

Wondering, the girl did as the fairy told her. She asked her mother for the goat's left hoof, and her mother let her have it. She had no idea

what the girl wanted with it, for what can you do with a hoof, which doesn't even have any meat to eat on it? That just showed what a stupid child Two Eyes was, thought her mother.

Two Eyes buried the hoof exactly where the fairy had said she must, and next morning, she saw a glittering tree outside her window. Its branches and leaves were made of silver, and golden apples hung on it. The tree had grown just where Two Eyes buried the goat's hoof.

Her mother and sisters couldn't understand it. They stared and stared in amazement.

What did it mean – could the child work magic? First a goat with a table full of food, now a tree with golden fruit! One Eye was the first to climb the tree and put out her hand for the shining apples. But the branches drew away from her, and she couldn't pick the fruit. However high she climbed, however hard she tried to pluck the apples, she could not get her hands on a single one.

Next Three Eyes climbed the tree. She felt sure she would succeed. I can see better than my sister, with my three eyes, she thought. But as soon as she came anywhere near an apple the branch moved, and suddenly the fruit was too high or too low for her to pick, too far to the

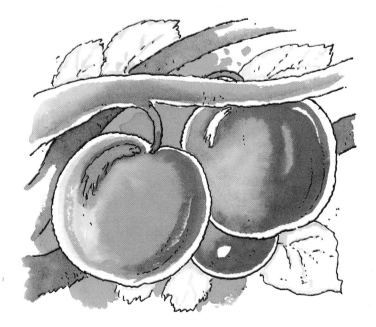

left or too far to the right. The girls' mother had no better luck. It was as if the apples were afraid of her, for as soon as she came near them they disappeared. Then, quietly, Two Eyes asked whether she might try. To the   great   surprise of the other three, the branches bent down to her, so that she could easily pick the apples and hardly had to climb any way up the tree at all. Soon her apron was full. When Two Eyes came back to her mother and sisters they greedily seized her apron and took all the apples she had picked away from her.

One day a prince rode past the house, and was amazed by the sight of the silver tree. One Eye and Three Eyes saw the rider rein in his horse and stop to look at it.
How handsome he looked sitting there on horse-back! One Eye and Three Eyes began offering him some of the golden apples, hoping that the prince would like them.
Whatever they did, however, they still could not touch any of the fruit.
Two Eyes, who had slipped out through the door, quickly climbed the tree and picked some of the apples. The prince gave her a friendly smile, and he saw that Two Eyes had a very pretty face. Without more ado, he asked her to go with him to the castle where he lived. Two Eyes told him how unhappy she was, and said she would gladly go with him, so the prince put her on his horse in front of him and galloped away to his castle.
The very next day the prince married Two Eyes, and a magnificent

wedding feast was held. There was dancing, and Two Eyes wore beautiful clothes and ate well at the feast.

From now on she led a much better life with her prince, who loved her dearly. Nor was the prince all she had, for her tree with the golden apples stood in a fine place in the castle garden. It had uprooted itself from the ground and followed Two Eyes to her new home.

Two Eyes took good care of the silver tree, and as long as she lived she polished the apples every day so that they shone in the sun.

One day two strange women came to the castle, knocked at the gate and begged for money. They looked very wretched; their clothes were dirty and ragged, and they were both thin as rakes. Two Eyes recognized them at once as her sisters, for one of them had only one eye and the other had three.

Although they had always been so unkind to Two Eyes, she felt sorry for them now.

Nothing had gone well for them since she went away with her prince. Their mother had died of starvation when there was nothing left to eat, and the two sisters went out into the world to beg. Two Eyes took them

into the castle with her, and she treated them well. So they all lived happily together: Two Eyes and her prince, the five children who were born to them, and even One Eye and Three Eyes.

Rumpelstiltskin

Once upon a time there was a miller who was very poor, and had nothing in the world but a beautiful daughter. He owned his mill too, of course, but he could grind only enough flour to bake a couple of loaves a day, and that was just enough for the two of them. However, the miller was a proud man, and did not want people to know he was poor, so everyone thought he earned plenty of money.

One day the king went driving through the land to see how his subjects were doing. Now and then the royal coach stopped, and the king himself got out, talked to someone, took a good look around, and then drove on again.

So he stopped to speak to the miller, who was hard at work in his mill. When the king asked how he was, the miller didn't want to admit that he could grind only enough flour to bake bread for himself, and he said: "Oh, I'm very well, your Majesty. I work hard in my mill, to be sure, but' that's no bad thing. What's more, I have a real treasure of a daughter! She's a most remarkable girl, for she can spin straw into gold. So you see, your Majesty, my daughter and I live very comfortably together here."

The king realized at once that this was a windfall. A girl who could spin straw into gold! You didn't find someone like that every day. And while the miller might be rich, he, the king, had troubles enough. His treasure chest was nearly always empty, and when a king has no money left, how can he rule his country? The king was not a happy man.

"If what you say is true," he said to the miller, "then you can bring your daughter to the palace tomorrow. I want to see what she can do."

When the miller had taken his daughter to the royal palace next morning, the king led her to a room full of straw. He sent for a spinning wheel, and said, "Get down to work at once, for if you haven't spun this straw into gold by early tomorrow morning you must die. I am your king, and I need the gold badly. And if your father was lying he will be

109

punished for it. No one may tell lies to the king."

So the king left the girl alone in the room full of straw. She heard the key turn in the lock, and there she was, shut in.

The poor child did not know what to do. She had never tried turning straw into gold before, and much as she wished to save her life, she had no idea how to set about obeying the king's orders.

So there she sat, and when hours seemed to have gone by, and yet not a bit of the straw had been turned into gold, she began to weep.

Then all of a sudden, quite unexpectedly, the door opened and in came a strange little man. He was a comical figure with his long beard and glittering eyes. He looked at her and he skipped up and down. "Good evening, miller's daughter," said he. "May I ask why you are so sad?"

The miller's daughter told him how she must spin straw into gold, and how of course she could do no such thing, for her father had merely been boasting.

"Nothing is impossible for someone with magic powers like mine," said the little man. "What will you give me if I spin the straw into gold for you?"

"I will give you my necklace," said the girl.

"Done," said the little man.

He went to the spinning wheel, set it whirring around, and in no time at all he had spun a couple of the big bundles of straw into a glowing spool of gold.

Then he fitted another spool on the spinning wheel. Whirr, went the wheel, and another great heap of straw was spun into gold. And so it went on all night. Long before the sun rose there was not a stalk of straw left. Gratefully, the miller's daughter gave the little man her necklace, and he immediately disappeared.

A little later the key turned in the door, and the king came into the room. How surprised and delighted he was to see that the straw had really been turned into gold!

However, he was not by any means satisfied yet. Now that he saw so much gold all in one place, he wanted even more. He had the girl taken to another room, much larger than the first, and it took four footmen two hours to stack the room full of all the straw they could find.

"Now, my dear," said the king, "if you love your life make sure this is all turned into gold by tomorrow morning. And if it isn't, you must die. I am your king and I need gold, and since I am lord of the land you must do as I say. So get down to work at once."

The door was locked, and there sat the miller's daughter. Once again she sat for hours, until there were tears in her eyes. She had hoped the strange little man would come back and help her, but all was still around her.

However, when the miller's daughter was in the deepest despair, all of a sudden there stood the little man in front of her.

"What will you give me if I spin this straw into gold?" he asked.

"My ring," she said. "It's all I have."

The little man was satisfied with that, and set to work. The spinning wheel whirred merrily around, and soon there were spools of gold stacked up where there had been only straw before. Within an hour all the straw was gone, the little man took the girl's ring, and in a twinkling he was gone. A strange little fellow he was, here one moment, gone again the next!

Then the king came in, and he was delighted to see all that gold. He had more than enough to last him a long time now; he was not poor any more.

Yet still he thought it was not enough. He sent for straw, even more of it than the first two times put together.

"See that it's all spun into gold by tomorrow morning," he said, "and if you don't do as I say you must die. But if you do it, then I will marry you and you will be queen."

For the king thought that the poor miller's daughter would be the richest bride he could find anywhere in the world. A girl who could spin straw into gold was always sure to be wealthy, and it would be a good idea to marry her. Besides, she was beautiful and good-natured too.

As soon as the king had left the room, there stood the little man. "What will you give me if I help you?" he asked.

"I have nothing left to give," replied the girl sadly. "I've already given you everything I owned."

"You will have plenty more once you are queen," said the little man, who seemed to know all about the king and his intention of marrying her.

"Yes, indeed," said the girl.

"Very well," said the little man. "Then I want the first child you have when you are queen!"

My first child, thought the girl; perhaps I won't have any children at all, and if I don't I'll have nothing to give this strange little man, so he'll have struck a bad bargain. And if I do have a child, the king will protect it.

In any case, she had no choice: she could see no other way out of her difficulty, so she had to agree to what the little man asked.

She nodded her consent, and the little man went to work at once. He spun and he spun, and the wheel went merrily around. The straw flew through his fingers, and he had finished even faster than the other two times. The room shone with all the gold in it, and this time, at last, the king was satisfied.

"I have gold enough for the time being," he said, "and if I do want more it's soon made. But now let us be married."

And so they were. Servants rode through the land spreading the news of the king's wedding. Kings and queens of many other countries came to the palace, where the king and the miller's daughter were married with great ceremony.

Everyone admired the king for giving his heart to a simple girl of his own people, not a foreign princess.

A year later a child was born to the king and queen: a little princess. The whole country rejoiced. The baby was a sweet little girl who soon learned to laugh.

The queen had not given the strange little man and her promise another thought. But the little man himself had not forgotten that he was to have the queen's first child in return for spinning straw into gold, and one day he suddenly appeared in the queen's bedroom.

"I have come for the child," he said. "It is mine now!"

The queen was terrified. She burst out sobbing and began promising the

little man anything he wanted, if only she might keep her baby. But the little man refused everything she offered. He did not need money or treasures, for he could make them himself if he wanted to, as no one knew better than the queen. She also knew that the little princess was worth more than all the treasures and all the money in the world to her mother.

However, when the queen went down on her knees, at her wits' end with fear and grief, and begged him to let her keep her child, the little man seemed to feel some pity for her.

"Very well," he said, "I will give you three days' grace. If you can guess what my name is by the end of those three days, you may keep your child."

With these words, the little man disappeared. The queen began making long lists of names, and she sent messengers out through the land to find more.

When the little man came back next day she began asking if his name was Tom, or Dick, or Harry, and when the little man shook his head she spent two hours naming all the names she had written down. But at

every name the little man shook his head, and every time he said, "No, that's not my name."

Next day she had more lists of names ready, and to be on the safe side she had included a great many strange ones, for how could you know with an odd little man like this one?

However, the little man's name was not Longbeard, Lickpot or Lopears. Nor was he called Spindleshanks or Spiderweb or Stickylugs. He kept shaking his head when she asked if his name was Bobbleguts or Babblemouth or Bellylaugh.

"No, that's not my name," was the answer every time. And when the queen could think of no more names he turned to leave.

"But I'll be back tomorrow," said the little man, "so you must guess my name by then, for if you don't your time is up."

Now the queen was really frightened. Guessing a name had seemed so easy, but it was turning out dreadfully difficult.

She was still racking her brain for more names when one of the messengers she had sent out came back, and told her he had not been able to discover any new names, but he had seen a very strange sight. And he told her his story.

He had come upon a little hut in a dense forest close to a high mountain. There was a fire burning brightly outside the house. He had seen a very strange little man capering around the fire as if he were dancing for joy, and singing a little song as he danced. The messenger had remembered the song, and he repeated it to the queen:

Today I brew, tomorrow I bake,
next day the queen's dear child I'll take.
How lucky for me she never will claim
that Rumpelstiltskin is my name!

The queen thanked the messenger with all her heart, and as soon as he was out of the room and had closed the door behind him she began dancing and singing for joy herself. Now at last, she felt sure, she had the right name!

Just as he had done before, the little man suddenly appeared before her. "Well, queen, do you know my name – or haven't you been able to think of anything this time?" he asked.

"Why, of course I know your name!" laughed the queen. "Aren't you called Robin? That is a good name for a man who lives in the woods!"

But the little man grinned and shook his head. "I'm sorry, queen," he said, "but that's not my name, I promise you!"

The queen pretended to be deep in thought. "Then maybe your name is John. Yes, it must be John!"

"Ah, but it isn't! I'm not called John," the little man told her. "You had better give up, for you will never guess. Well, you may try once again. Guess just once more, and then ... "
He looked meaningly at the cradle.
"Then can your name be ... Rumpelstiltskin?" asked the queen.
"The devil must have told you that! The devil must have told you that!" shrieked the little man, stamping his foot, and he stamped so hard that his right leg sank into the ground right up to the knee. That made him so angry that he took his left leg in both hands, and he tugged so hard that he pulled himself in two.

And then he disappeared as suddenly as he had come. The queen never had any more trouble from the greedy little man, and the princess grew up happily with her mother in the palace, where they both lived happily ever after.

The Fisherman and his Wife

Down by the sea among the sand dunes there stood a little hut, and a fisherman lived there with his wife. The fisherman liked his life. He loved the sea, and went off whistling every day to catch fish. On the way he talked to the little rabbits he met, and he waved to the birds flying high in the blue sky. But the fisherman's wife did not like living there at all. She hated their little hut, and wished she had a big house with servants, and wardrobes full of clothes. However, the fisherman did not have enough money for such things. He worked hard, fishing all day long. He caught enough to feed the two of them well every day, but not enough to get rich.

Meanwhile, the fisherman's wife tried to raise some vegetables in the garden beside their little hut, but it wasn't easy, for not much would grow there so close to the sea.

One day the fisherman went out at dawn as usual to his place on the rocks. He looked cheerfully around him. The sun was just rising, and it was going to be a beautiful day again. He was glad he didn't have to stay indoors all day! And with a little luck, he would catch more fish than yesterday.

Untiringly, he cast his line out into the blue waves, but he kept hauling it in again empty. The crabs ate up the scraps of dough he used as bait, and there were never any fish on the hook. After a couple of hours the fisherman began to feel anxious. He must catch something soon, for otherwise he would go home empty-handed, and then there would be nothing at all to eat in the evening, and his wife would be angry.

As he sat thinking like this, the rod suddenly bent, and exerting all his strength, the fisherman hauled up a gigantic fish. He had never seen such a huge creature at the end of his line before. In astonishment, he gazed at the great fish, and then he started back in alarm – for this fish could speak!

Amazed, the fisherman heard it say:

*I beg you, spare my life today
and your kindness I'll repay.*

The fisherman immediately did as he was asked: he carefully took the hook out of the fish's mouth and let the creature drop back into the water. The fish swam swiftly out to the open sea, darting through the water like a flash of silver lightning, and was lost from sight.

Still spellbound by his adventure, the fisherman went home to tell his wife about it, but she was furious. She was so tired of being a poor fisherman's wife that she had grown very dissatisfied with her life.

When the fisherman had told his tale, she immediately began shouting and screaming at him. "You fool!" she cried. "How could you let such an opportunity slip?"

The fisherman looked at her, his eyes wide with puzzlement, for he did not understand what she meant.

"Didn't you stop to think that if such a fish can talk, it can surely work magic too? You ought never to have let it go until it had granted you a wish. I am sure the fish could have done anything you asked! You're a fool, a stupid fisherman without a bit of sense in your head!"

"Oh, do be quiet!" said her husband. "The fish swam away out to sea, and it must be well away by now. I'm sure it's forgotten what it said."

But his wife was still angry, and she scolded him so much that the poor fisherman was almost deafened, and finally agreed to do as she asked.

"Very well," he said. "I'll go back to the fish, but what do you want? What am I to wish for?"

"A house, a big house with beautiful furniture," said his wife, "and a garden, and a henhouse, and a … "

The fisherman did not stop to hear what else she wanted, but went back to the place where he always fished.

Cupping his hands around his mouth, he called as loud as he could to the fish swimming somewhere out in the deep water. "Fish, fish, are you still there?"

Almost at once the waves began to surge and roar, and the fish put its head above the water and asked what the matter was.

"I told my wife what happened," said the fisherman, "and she thinks you can work magic. She wants me to ask you for a better house in return for putting you back into the sea. We are very poor, and my wife is unhappy because we've lived in such a little hut so long."

The fish looked at the fisherman, swam a little further out, opened its mouth and said:

As I am a magic fish
this time I will grant your wish.

No sooner had the fish spoken these words than it swam down beneath the waves again. Hardly believing it, the fisherman went back to his hut ... but the hut wasn't there any more! A fine house stood in its place. The roof was covered with thick straw thatch, there were spotlessly clean curtains at the windows, and the house looked just as fine inside as outside, with handsome cupboards and comfortable chairs where the fisherman could take a nap.

The fisherman was glad he had done as his wife wanted, for he was very happy with the change himself. This was certainly better than living in their shabby old hut!

For a few days the fisherman's wife seemed satisfied with her new house, but one evening she said to her husband, "This house is not as good as I thought. The kitchen garden is too small, and it doesn't get enough sun. No vegetables will grow there. And I'm tired of doing the housework and looking after the fowls in the poultry yard."

"You are not very grateful," said the fisherman. "We've been so lucky! Other fishermen have nothing but a little hut without windows or doors, and here we are, warm and comfortable, sheltered from the wind and the rain. We can get vegetables from the garden, the chickens give us eggs and meat, and we have enough to eat every day!"

"What a great dunderhead you are!" said the fisherman's wife. "Why don't we ask the fish for something else? We only have to make a wish and it will be granted. It would be very stupid of us not to make another wish, and as for you, you're even more of a fool than I thought. I don't just want an ordinary house. I want a castle like the prince's, a real castle with towers and servants and a drawbridge in front of it."

And whatever the fisherman said, it was no use. His wife scolded him so much that in the end he gave way, although he felt very unhappy about it. When he had gone back to the place where he always fished, he called the fish. He was sure that it would merely laugh when he told it about his wife's extraordinary wish. Surely it would never help him this time. However, once again the water roared and surged, and when the fisherman had asked for a castle the fish said, in friendly tones:

Well, as I am a magic fish,
once again I'll grant your wish.

When the fisherman came home to the place where his house had stood, it was gone. A magnificent castle stood there instead, with towers and a drawbridge, and flags waving in the breeze everywhere. The castle looked very grand. The fisherman went in through a great gate, and arm in arm with his wife he walked through all the rooms.
Each hall they passed through was finer than the last. There were mirrors everywhere, and crystal chandeliers; the furniture was covered with expensive fabric, there were tapestries on the walls, and the tables and chests were laden with gold and silver dishes and gleaming porcelain. They stared and stared.

However, they had not finished yet, for a castle has other buildings belonging to it, and the fish had provided them too. There were stables full of horses, a farm and a park, and they were greeted by a great many farm workers, servants and gardeners who bowed low to the fisherman and his wife.

One day the fisherman, wishing to please his wife, asked her, "Well, are you happy now at last? You look like a queen!"

"A queen! A queen ... well, I'm not a queen, but I would like to be!" said the fisherman's wife. "Why didn't I think of that before? I am sure the fish can make me a queen by magic. Go back to it at once and tell it what I want. Hurry up, don't stand there dawdling!"

And it was all just as it had been before: whatever the fisherman said, his wife refused to listen. He had to go back to the sea and see whether the fish would come when it was called.

Sure enough, once again the fish put its head out of the water, and before the fisherman had said so much as a word, the fish told him:

Well, as I am a magic fish,
once again I'll grant your wish.

When the fisherman came home there sat his wife on a throne, surrounded by knights and courtiers. She really did look like a queen, even if she was rather fat: she wore a magnificent dress, and a golden crown on her head, and rich necklaces and bracelets and rings.

The fisherman shook his head. He couldn't make it out. Why did his wife want more and more all the time? Would she be happy at last now? She had plenty of servants to carry out her orders, bow low before her and do all the work about the great castle, so perhaps she might finally be satisfied. It was not long, however, before the queen fell into a discontented mood again, and her temper became worse and worse. Feeling a little afraid of what he might hear in answer, the fisherman asked her, "Why are you so sad?"

"I am sad because my kingdom is too small," said the fisherman's wife. "I'd really like to be empress. An empress is more important than a queen. That's it, that's why I'm so sad! Hurry up, you fool, go and tell the fish to make me empress."

This time the fisherman dared not go back to the fish. He had put it back into the sea only once, and now the fish had granted many, many wishes for him. The fisherman was ashamed because his wife was never happy, but it was no use, once again she made him go back to the sea. So there he stood on the beach again, and he heard a voice coming from the waves:

Well, as I am a magic fish,
once again I'll grant your wish.

When the fisherman saw that the fish had granted his wishes yet again, he said to his wife, who had become empress: "You must stop now, for you can't rise any higher. You are empress, and everyone does what you want. You have everything you ever wished for: a fine castle, plenty of money, servants and beautiful clothes, so now you must be content."

However, the fisherman's wife knew there was someone even more important than herself. The Pope was more important than any empress, so now she wanted to be Pope. The fisherman was horrified, for this was going too far.

"You can't be Pope!" he cried. "There's already a Pope, and there can't be two at once. This time the fish will be angry and think I'm out of my mind."

But still the fish was not angry, and once again the fisherman's wife had her wish. When the fisherman came home, there was his wife, and she was Pope. All the kings and emperors, princes and princesses in the

world were bowing down to her, but still it wasn't enough. The fisherman's wife wanted to be God!

"Please, wife," begged the fisherman, "that's impossible. Just think about it, and be satisfied with all you have."

But the fisherman's wife was angrier than she had ever been before. She threw a golden vase at the fisherman's head and shouted, "Go back to the fish, great fool that you are!"

Very sorrowfully, the fisherman went down to the beach, and now a terrible storm rose. Sand whirled through the air, and the waves lashed the shore.

The fisherman crawled down to the water's edge on hands and knees and called softly for the fish, for he dared not call aloud. But the fish did not appear. After a while the storm died down, and the fisherman went home again. He was badly afraid. What would happen now?

Then he saw his house. Although it was not exactly a house … for where the Pope's palace had stood only a few hours before, there was now a tiny fisherman's hut, even smaller than the hut where the fisherman and his wife used to live. And the fisherman's wife was standing outside the hut in her patched, shabby clothes.

The fisherman did not really think the change was so bad. He would rather be a fisherman than live in a great palace. And as for the fisherman's wife – well, all her life she never learned to be satisfied with what she had.

The Golden Goose

Once upon a time there was a man who had three sons. Two of the sons were clever but one, the youngest, was stupid, or if perhaps he wasn't quite such a fool as he looked, everyone called him Stupid just the same. As a child, Stupid was never allowed to join his brothers' games, and later on his father hardly ever gave him any important work to do, so that he was trusted only with the boring, dirty work about the place. Stupid was always being teased as well – by his father, his brothers and even his mother, who thought him a simpleton as well.

One day the young men's father had cut down a large tree in the forest, and now it all had to be chopped into pieces.

"Off you go and chop the tree up," the father told his eldest son, and his mother gave him a bottle of wine and a big, crisp cake she had baked to take with him.

So the eldest son set off. After walking some way he came to the outskirts of the forest, and there he saw a little old man sitting on a tree trunk to the left of the path. The man said a friendly, "Good day."

"Will you let me have a bit of your cake and a sip of your wine?" asked the little man. "I'm fainting with hunger and thirst. All I need is a tiny crumb and a little drop."

But the young man said, "If I share my food and drink with you I'll have nothing left, and then I'll perish of hunger myself!" He didn't want to give the little man anything, and so he just walked on.

Soon he came to the place where his father had cut down the tree, and a mighty tree it was! There was plenty of work to be done, and the lad set about it at once. He took his hatchet and raised it to bring it down hard on the wood, but he cut his leg instead.

"Ouch!" he cried, for he had hurt himself badly and his leg was bleeding. He was unable to chop any more wood, so he staggered home as best he could, not knowing that the little man whose request he had refused had caused his injury.

"I've hurt my leg!" said the eldest son when he finally reached home.

"You're as bad as your youngest brother!" said his father crossly. "I can't trust you to do anything."

He called for his second son and told him, "You'll have to do your elder brother's work. I cut down a tree in the forest, and you must go and chop it up."

So the second son set off, taking a delicious cake and a bottle of wine with him, and he went on his way whistling. He found a little old man sitting just where the path led into the forest, the same little man who had made the eldest brother cut his own leg.

"I can hardly walk another step, and I'm so hungry and thirsty. Won't you give me something to eat and drink?" he asked the second brother.

"No," said the young man. "I'm still growing, and you're old! I'm not going to waste my delicious cake and wine on you!" And without another word to the little man, the second brother went into the wood.

He soon saw the tree lying there, and decided to set to work at once. He struck the wood with his hatchet as hard as ever he could, but a big splinter flew into his leg and stuck there.

"Ouch!" cried the young man. Once again, his injury was the little old man's doing, although he didn't know it.

Since he couldn't go on chopping wood, the young man went home again, and his father was very angry with him.

"What's all this nonsense?" shouted the father furiously. "Can't you even chop up a tree? I suppose I'll have to do it myself, since you two are so useless!"

"Father," said his youngest son quietly, "why don't you send me?"

"You?" laughed his father. "I'm not giving such important work to a stupid lad like you. If your brothers can't do it, then you never will."

"I could try, all the same," suggested Stupid.

His father lost his temper. "No, I won't hear of it!"

But his son insisted and insisted, and eventually the father gave in and said, "Oh, very well, you can try. There'll be trouble if you don't succeed, though."

Stupid's mother gave him a crust of bread and a bottle of sour beer. She thought it would be a waste to give her stupid son a delicious cake and

a bottle of good wine to take with him. Stupid didn't mind, for he was used to nothing better.

He set off cheerfully along the path, and just like his two brothers before him, he saw the little old man sitting on the outskirts of the forest. The little man greeted him, and said, "I'm fainting with hunger and thirst. Will you give me something to eat?"

Stupid was sorry for the old man. "All I have is some stale bread and sour beer," he said. "But if that will do, let's share it."

"You're a good young fellow," said the old man gratefully.

Stupid took his crust of bread and bottle of beer out of his bag. But a very strange thing had happened: the bread had become a beautiful cake, and the sour beer had turned into a bottle of the best wine. Stupid and the little man ate as much as they could hold.

Then the old man thanked Stupid again. "You have a kind heart," he said, "and so I will reward you. Chop down the old oak over there, and you'll find something of value among its roots."

Stupid was curious to find out what the old man meant. He immediately chopped down the tree the little man had pointed out, and among the

130

roots he saw something glittering. He dug his fingers into the sand, and then he saw that it was a goose with feathers of pure gold, shining in the sunlight. Stupid thought the golden goose was beautiful.

He decided not to go home again. He had a golden goose now, and he was sure she would help him to earn his living, for a goose like that must be worth a great deal of money.

So he left the forest and went to an inn, planning to spend the night there.

Now the innkeeper had three daughters, and they all wondered what kind of strange bird the young man had brought with him.

"When he isn't looking, I'll pull out one of its feathers," said one of the daughters.

So when Stupid had gone out for a breath of fresh air, the girl went to his room. She stared at the goose in amazement, and tried to pull out a feather, but she failed, for her hand stuck fast to the goose! It might have been glued to the bird, and whatever she did, she couldn't free herself.

The innkeeper's second daughter was feeling curious too.

"Where can my sister be?" she said to herself, and she decided to go and take a look. So she went to Stupid's room, and there she saw her sister.

"Don't touch that goose or you'll be stuck!" said the eldest daughter. She tried to push her sister away with her free hand – but her hand stuck to the other girl, and she couldn't get that hand free either.

The innkeeper's youngest daughter came to look too. "Go away, go away, don't touch us!" cried her sisters, but too late. The youngest daughter had already touched her sister's hand.

So there stood the three sisters, stuck to each other and the goose. However hard they tried, they couldn't break free, and they had to spend the whole night like that.

In the morning Stupid rose early. "I've a long way to go today," he said, and without more ado he picked up his goose and left the inn. He was still so sleepy that he never noticed the three girls stuck to his goose. Whether the girls liked it or not, they had to run after Stupid, and a hard time they had, for they kept tripping over each other's legs, and besides, Stupid set a brisk pace, so they had to move fast.

They came to a village, and the minister of the village church saw them. "Hey there, where are you going?" he cried, and he ran after the girls and the young man.

"We're stuck to each other!" cried the girls.

"I'll soon free you," said the minister, and he took the hand of the youngest girl, who was at the back. So then he was stuck too!

"Help, help!" cried the minister. "I'm stuck! Get me free!"

Then the verger of the church came running up.

"What's all this, sir?" cried the verger. "You haven't forgotten you're taking a christening service this morning, have you? Surely you aren't running away with three strange girls and a young man, sir?" And he took the minister's arm, so then he was stuck fast himself.

A little later they met two farmers on their way to the fields with their spades over their shoulders.

"Help, help!" cried the verger. "We're being kidnapped!"

And before they knew it, the two farmers were stuck fast too.

By now there was quite a procession following Stupid. More and more people kept joining him. Before long the village baker, two schoolgirls, the mayor's wife and three policemen had been trapped as well.

They would soon be coming to the capital city, where the palace of the king who ruled that country stood. The king had an only daughter, a beautiful, clever girl, but there was just one thing wrong with her: she never laughed. She didn't like jokes or funny stories, and she looked on the dark side of everything.

The king wished she were more cheerful, for after all, she would be queen one day, and a queen mustn't always be looking cross.

"You see, one of your subjects might give you a nice bottle of wine on your birthday," the king told his daughter, "and then you have to smile and say thank you, even if you'd rather have had something else." But nothing did any good. Every day the princess looked as gloomy as ever. The king had promised that any man who could make his daughter laugh could marry her, for he would give anything to see her smile.

Stupid and his followers came into the city and went along the main street leading to the king's palace.

"Just look at that!" said everyone. "What a funny procession!" And they couldn't help laughing, for it certainly was a strange sight to see all those people running after one another. More and more onlookers came up: men, women and children and even animals.

The princess was standing on her balcony when the procession reached the palace. First came Stupid with his golden goose, after him the three girls, and finally all the others. It was such a comical sight that the princess couldn't help laughing. First she just smiled, but then she began laughing harder and harder, until she was laughing so much that she almost fell off the balcony. Back at home in his village, Stupid had heard the story of the princess, and he knew that now he had made her laugh he could marry her. The king was glad his daughter could laugh at last, but now he regretted the bargain he had made, for he didn't want to see his daughter married to a man called Stupid.

So he thought of a way out. He summoned Stupid and told him, "You must drink my whole wine cellar dry before you marry my daughter. If you can do that, you are worthy to be her husband. You may take a friend to help you, but the two of you must drink every drop in the cellar." Stupid immediately thought of the little man in the forest, and he went off at once. Luckily there was no one following him now, for he had left the goose behind. At that very moment, in fact, the blacksmith was hard at work trying to melt the spot where the girls were still stuck fast to the goose, and of course he had to go very carefully, so it would be quite a while before they were free again.

So Stupid reached the outskirts of the forest, and there sat the little old man on a bench beside the path where it ran into the woods. Stupid told him what the problem was.

"And now I have to drink the king's whole wine cellar dry," he finished. "It's a huge cellar, stacked with barrels from floor to ceiling!"

"I'll go with you, for I'm thirsty enough!" said the little man, and they set off for the palace together.

"I wish you luck, gentlemen!" said the king to Stupid and the little old man as they stood at the door of the wine cellar. And he held the door open for them, smiling. Well, he had come off lightly! The two of them could never drink his whole cellar dry, and so his daughter wouldn't have to marry Stupid.

Stupid and the little man went in and looked around. Barrels full of the choicest wines stood along all the walls, hundreds and hundreds of barrels, row by row. And the old man immediately began to drink.

He drank and he drank and he drank. It took him all day, but as evening approached the end was in sight. And lo and behold, by nightfall he had drunk up all the wine to the very last drop.

"The wine is finished," Stupid told the king, "so now I'd like to be married to your daughter."

"No, that won't do," said the king, in great alarm. "First you must eat up all the grain in my granary. I'll have it baked into bread tonight."

And that night all the ovens in the city were alight, baking bread. All the grain in the king's granary was used up, and by evening a great mountain of loaves stood in the square outside the palace.

"Off you go," said the king.

Luckily the little old man was very hungry, and he began to eat. Loaf after loaf went down his throat, for it seemed there was no satisfying his hunger. The little man went on eating and eating until he had finally eaten the very last loaf, and there was not a single crumb left for the birds.

Now the king could not object any more. Stupid had carried out three tasks: he had made the king's daughter laugh, and he had done two impossible things as well, for the king knew of no one else who could drink so much wine and eat so much bread.

"Very well," he told the young man, sighing. "You may marry my daughter."

The wedding was held the very next day, and that evening there was a magnificent feast at the palace.

A few years later the old king died. Stupid came to the throne, he and his wife ruled the country for many years, and he was a good, wise king, so that everyone in the country loved him.

The Twelve Dancing Princesses

Once upon a time there was a king who had twelve daughters, all as beautiful as each other. The first had lovely black hair, the second had big blue eyes, the third had the prettiest cherry lips in the whole world, the fourth had a skin as soft as satin. In fact anyone who saw them would say at once, "Do you see those princesses? I don't believe I ever set eyes on such beautiful girls before."

They all slept together in a great room where their beds stood side by side. They liked the company better than having a room each, and it meant that when the lights were put out in the evening they could talk to one another before going to sleep. They had slept together as children, and so it had gone on, for all twelve girls were good friends and told each other all their secrets.

Every evening, when the twelve beautiful princesses had gone to bed, the king would shut the door of their bedroom and bolt it. He had been doing that for quite a long time, and there was something he could not understand: when he drew back the bolt in the morning and the door was opened, he always saw that their shoes were worn out. Not just one pair of shoes, or even two: no, all twelve pairs of shoes had been worn into holes overnight. Of course the king asked his daughters how their shoes could wear out while they lay in bed asleep. However, the princesses just looked at him, smiled sweetly and offered not a word of explanation. Yes, it was certainly strange how those shoes wore out, they said, but they really had no idea how it happened.

"No, Father, we don't understand it either, but of course we're tucked comfortably up in bed and fast asleep," said the youngest daughter at last, and that was all they ever said to the king about the shoes that were worn into holes.

Well, one day the king sat on his great golden throne thinking hard, and because he was a clever king he had clever ideas. What makes shoes wear out, the king wondered, and what do twelve beautiful princesses like to do best? Of course he knew that: princesses love to dance. So what were his daughters doing when the king thought they were lying tucked up in bed asleep? They must be dancing.

When he had thought all this out, the king made it known that anyone who discovered where the princesses went to dance at night could marry one of them, and besides that the man who found out the secret could become king later. But anyone who tried to solve the puzzle must do it quickly, for he would be allowed only three days, and if he didn't find the solution within three days then he would be executed.

Soon a prince came knocking at the gate wanting to try his luck. You never know, thought the prince, perhaps he might succeed, and he liked the idea of being married to one of the king's beautiful daughters. The prince was given a hearty welcome, and in the evening the servants led him to a bedroom next to the great room where the princesses slept. There was a bed made up for him, and from the place where it stood he could keep watch, and perhaps discover where the princesses went to dance. The door of his room was left open so that the princesses could do nothing and go nowhere without being seen by the prince. He could hear every little sound and see every movement they made.

However, the prince's eyelids grew heavy, and he fell asleep. When he woke up in the morning the princesses had been dancing, for the soles of their shoes were worn into holes. Exactly the same thing happened on the two following nights, and then the prince's head was cut off without mercy.

Many other princes and strong, clever young men came to try their luck too, but none of them found out the secret of the twelve princesses, and after three days and three nights they all had their heads cut off, even though the poor young men had done their best.

One day a soldier who had been wounded in the wars and had to leave the army came walking down the road to the city where the king and his dancing daughters lived. The young soldier met an old woman who asked where he was going.

"I don't really know," said the soldier, and he added, as a joke, that he wouldn't mind finding out what the princesses did at night. "Then perhaps I can marry one of them and become king!"

"Well, there's no reason why not," said the old woman, "just so long as you don't drink any of the wine they bring you, and pretend to be fast asleep." So saying, she gave him a short cape, and the soldier listened carefully as she added, "When you put on this cape you will be invisible, so you

can follow the twelve princesses and discover where they go by night. But be careful, for they are very clever!"

When the kind old woman had given the soldier this good advice, he began to think about it seriously. In the end he plucked up his courage, went to the king and said that he would like to try finding out the princesses' secret. The king looked at the soldier, and thought it was a pity that this fine young man was sure to have his head cut off when three days were up, for many brave princes had failed, and so would the soldier. And yet you never know – so the soldier was allowed his chance. That evening, when it was time for bed, the servants took him to the room next to the princesses' bedroom. He was just about to go to bed when the eldest princess came in and brought him a goblet of wine. She smiled sweetly at him and said, "Well, soldier, since you want to sit up all night, I'm sure you can do with a glass of wine. Drink it up and it will put heart into you."

The soldier thanked her kindly, and pretended to be draining the whole goblet at once. However, he had fastened a sponge under his chin and let the wine run down into it, so that he didn't drink a drop. Then he lay

down and kept quite still for a while, closing first one eye and then the other, and he began to snore aloud. The twelve princesses heard him and laughed.

Then they got up, opened their wardrobes and took out their prettiest dresses. They made themselves pretty, chattering all the time and enjoying themselves. They were looking forward to going dancing, and there lay the soldier snoring like a dragon spitting fire. What a noise he made!

But the youngest princess was quieter than her sisters this evening. "I have a feeling that something is going to happen to us," she said. "Some kind of misfortune!"

"You silly goose!" said the eldest princess. "You're always scared of something! Have you forgotten how many clever princes have tried in vain to discover our secret? I hardly even needed to give that silly soldier a potion to make him drowsy – he's sleeping like a log! Don't you hear him?"

The youngest princess shook her head to rid herself of her uneasy thoughts. Of course her eldest sister must be right, for what could go wrong? Yet why was her mind still not at rest?

When they were all ready, wearing their prettiest dresses and with their hair beautifully arranged, they took another look at the soldier, but he was lying in bed, never moving, with his eyes tightly closed.

Now the eldest princess knew for sure that all was safe. She went to one of the beds and tapped it. The bed sank down into the floor, and one by

one the girls disappeared through the trapdoor that opened. The soldier, who had seen everything, did not hesitate for a moment, but put on his cape and followed the youngest princess down the staircase under the floor. Halfway down the stairs he trod on the long silver train of her dress. She was frightened, and said, "What was that? Who took hold of my skirt?"

"Don't be so silly," said the eldest princess. "You must have caught it on a nail."

They went on down and down, and when they were deep underground the soldier found himself in a wonderful avenue full of flowers. All the leaves were made of glittering, shining silver.

I'd better bring something away with me as proof, thought the soldier, for otherwise the king will never believe what I say. So he broke off a beautiful silver branch, and the tree made a loud cracking sound.

"Something is the matter!" cried the youngest princess. "Did you hear that?"

"Our princes are firing shots of joy because we'll soon be with them, that's all," said the eldest princess.

Next they came to an avenue with trees where all the leaves were made of gold, and finally they came into a third avenue where all the leaves

were set with sparkling diamonds, and each time the soldier broke off a twig, one of gold and one of diamonds. And each time the tree gave a mighty crack, which frightened the youngest princess, but her eldest sister laughed at her and said, once again, that the princes were firing their guns because they were so pleased that the princesses would soon arrive. Now they went faster, until they came to a great lake. There were twelve little boats by the bank, and a handsome prince sat in each boat. They had been waiting for the princesses, and each prince took one of the girls in his boat. The soldier, whose cape still made him invisible, stepped into the boat carrying the youngest princess.

"It's strange," said her prince, "but this boat seems much heavier than usual. I can hardly get it moving!"

"Perhaps it's because of the hot weather," said the girl.

"Maybe," agreed the prince, but he did not really think so.

On the opposite bank of the lake stood a magnificent castle, brightly lit, with merry music playing inside it. They rowed over to the castle, went in, and each prince danced there with the princess he loved.

The soldier danced too, but no one saw him because he had his cape

on. When one of the princesses took a goblet of wine he drank it all up at once, so that it was empty when she put it to her lips. That made the youngest princess afraid, but the eldest kept saying that she mustn't be so silly, for nothing could be wrong. Weren't they enjoying themselves? Very well, then!

They danced almost all night, until three o'clock in the morning, and by then the soles of their shoes were danced into holes and they had to stop. The princes rowed them back across the lake, and this time the soldier went in the boat with the eldest princess.

The girls said goodbye to their princes on the bank, and promised to come back the following night. As they went back up the stairs and through the trapdoor, the soldier hurried ahead of them and lay down in bed. When the twelve princesses came slowly and wearily up the stairs, he began snoring loudly again, so that they said, "Well, we're safe enough from him! What a racket he makes, snoring like that!"

They took off their beautiful dresses, tidied everything away, put the shoes they had danced into holes under their beds and fell asleep.

Next morning the soldier decided to say nothing, for he wanted to see

all those wonderful things again. So he went with the princesses the second night, and the third night too. Everything happened exactly as it had the first time, and the princesses danced until their shoes were worn into holes. On the last night, the soldier brought a goblet away with him. Now he had his twigs of silver, gold and diamond, and a goblet as proof of what he said as well.

At the end of the third night one of the king's servants came to tell the soldier that the king was expecting him. The soldier took his three twigs and his goblet and went before the king.

The twelve princesses were standing behind the door, listening. They thought that in one way it was a pity all those princes and brave young men had lost their lives, but in another way they were always glad their secret had not been discovered.

Today, however, when the king asked where his daughters danced their shoes into holes every night, the soldier told him about the underground passage, the boats that rowed across the lake and the castle, and then he showed his proof: the three twigs and the goblet.

The king immediately summoned his daughters, and asked if the soldier

had been telling the truth. The girls all realized that their secret was out after all, and they admitted it. "Yes, what the soldier said is true!" they said. Then the king asked the soldier which of his daughters he would like to marry, and the soldier chose the eldest princess, because she was about the same age as himself.

The wedding was celebrated that very day, and a magnificent feast it was, with as much dancing as the princesses had enjoyed every night in their secret castle. The king, who was growing old and felt tired of reigning, promised the soldier that he would soon be king himself, and so he was. All the other eleven princesses found handsome princes to marry, which was not very easy, for so many princes had been beheaded that there weren't many left. As for the soldier and the eldest princess, in time they had twelve little princes of their own, and the soldier was a good, just, wise king who ruled the country until he was very old.

Mount Semsi

Long ago two brothers lived in a little village that lay tucked away in a deep valley between high mountains. The two brothers grew up, and they both married, and they both had children. Each brother lived in a house of his own, but their houses were very different. The elder brother was very rich, but the younger brother was just a poor farmer who had to live on what his land would provide, and sometimes that was so little that the poor man could give his wife and children nothing to eat but what grew in their garden. Then he had no fruit or vegetables to sell, and so they could buy no meat or milk, but the poor farmer was happy, because he had a good wife and he loved his children. He wasn't even envious of his brother, who could buy anything he liked every day. The rich brother's children never went hungry, and they had beautiful clothes and as many fine toys as they wanted.

One day the poor brother was driving his cart through a great, wild forest. He was on his way to market, and he had taken a path he did not know because he thought it would be a short cut. But now that he looked around him he saw that he had never been here before. He hoped he would not be lost, and decided to take good notice of the way he went, so that he could get safely home again.

Then all of a sudden, right in front of him, he saw a mountain with bare, steep sides. It looked very wild and dangerous, and he was sure he had never seen this mountain before either. In surprise, he reined in the mule pulling his cart to make it stop. The animal's knees bent, and it looked back at its master with a reproachful expression. It wasn't used to such rough treatment, for the poor farmer was always very kind to it, and now it was alarmed and surprised.

The farmer sat there in his cart, staring at the unknown mountain, until he suddenly heard the sound of raised voices. Now it so happened that there were often thieves and robbers roaming these wild forests. The cautious farmer quickly hid his mule and cart in the bushes, then he climbed a tree. He sat on a stout branch, where he could see everything going on beneath him, but nobody could see him.

He had taken refuge on his branch just in time, for a few minutes later twelve grim-looking men came along the path and right up to the bare mountain. When they came to the first rocks they suddenly began calling, "Mount Semsi, open up! Mount Semsi, open up!"

And to the silent astonishment of the farmer, the mountain wall opened up. From his branch, the farmer could see a great cavern inside, and the company of robbers – for robbers they surely were – made their way in. Immediately the great wall of rock closed again.

A few minutes later the men appeared once more, but this time they were carrying big sacks. Then they called out, "Mount Semsi, close! Mount Semsi, close!"

The mountain closed again, leaving no sign of anything like a door, and the twelve men went away along the path. You could tell that the sacks they were carrying had been used many times, but what for?

When they had disappeared from sight, the farmer stayed on his branch for a little while, thinking. How he longed to take a look inside the cave with the magic entrance! But a tiny remnant of caution held him back. The sight of the twelve robbers' guns scared him so much that, curious as he might be about the rock that opened and closed of itself, he dared not look inside just yet.

So he waited a little longer, looking around him to make sure there was no one near. Then he slid down the tree trunk and went to the mountain

wall. A few paces away from the first rocks he stopped and called out loud, "Mount Semsi, open up! Mount Semsi, open up!"

And lo and behold, once again the bare mountain opened as if the door had been pulled back on a string, and the farmer was able to walk through the opening and into the cave. Immediately thousands of little lights met his eyes, dazzling him, for the cave was full of shining things: piles of gold and silver, the pale sparkle of diamonds, the glitter of jewels stacked in crates or scattered carelessly on the ground. The farmer had never seen so many precious things before, and the sight made him quite dizzy.

Shaking with excitement, there stood the farmer in the robbers' secret den, where they hid the rich loot they had stolen. They must go out robbing and stealing very often, and everything they had stolen lay here in this cave which the farmer had found by accident.

The poor farmer hesitated. Could he take away some of this precious treasure, just a little of it? He thought of his wife and his children, and how much they would like something good to eat, and he thought how nice it would be if he could afford fine clothes for his daughters. Then

he stuffed his pockets with gold, but he left the diamonds and jewels alone. Once he was outside the cave again, the farmer called, "Mount Semsi, close! Mount Semsi, close!"

He drove back home in his mule-cart in very high spirits. He made his wife and children happy with the gold, and even gave some away to the poor people of the village.

When the gold was all gone, he went to his brother to borrow a wooden measure almost as big as a bucket. He went off to the cave again, filled the measure with gold but left the jewels alone, and once more he was able to live well for several weeks. He bought presents for his wife and children, and they were all very happy.

Once again, when the gold was all gone, he went back to his rich elder brother to borrow the wooden measure. It was useful, for he could carry a good deal of gold away all at once in a big measure like that.

His brother, who had an envious nature, looked sourly at the farmer. Where was his younger brother getting all his money? These days he was giving his wife and daughters presents and buying everything he wanted. Indeed he, the elder brother, wasn't the richest man in the village any

more, and what really annoyed him was the fact that he had no idea where his younger brother's sudden wealth came from. However, the farmer knew his elder brother very well, and that was why he took good care not to give away the secret of his good fortune.

"I sold my grain at a good price," the farmer told his envious brother, "so lend me your measure again. I have to take some seed-corn to a farmer nearby who wants to grow grain as good as mine. All the farmers would like such good grain, so I'll make money out of it."

Without saying a word, the elder brother gave him the wooden measure. Then he tried to follow the farmer, hiding in the bushes. But now his younger brother had not one but two strong mules harnessed to his cart, and he drove away in a cloud of dust, cheerfully cracking his whip, and had soon disappeared over the horizon.

The rich brother went home in a bad temper. He sat by the fire and tried to think of a way to discover the truth. Next time he must manage to make his brother say where he was getting all that money!

Meanwhile, our farmer had filled the measure with golden coins a couple of times and gone home, still without touching the priceless

jewels. He knew he had better not take any of them, for if he did everyone would wonder how he came by such magnificent things. Then he would be followed, and the robbers might hear of it ... no, that would never do!

Surely, he thought, I'm doing no harm by making my wife and children happy and giving money away in the village. There are so many people in need, and I can help them a little. There are a great many poor people, and now I can give them a few gold coins! If I can do that, it must be a good thing, and it makes me very happy.

So the farmer drove home again in good spirits, and once more there was plenty of money in the farmhouse for a while.

But when he went back to his elder brother for a third time to borrow the measure, the man had cunningly smeared the bottom of the measure with sticky honey, and when the measure was given back the rich brother found a golden coin sticking to it. He went straight to his brother and asked, "What were you using my measure for?"

"Seed-corn, to be sure," replied the younger brother, suspecting nothing.

Then his brother showed him the golden coin, and threatened to tell everyone his younger brother was a common thief if he didn't tell the truth. The farmer was afraid, and told the whole tale of his adventure, describing the place where the robbers had their den. The elder brother laughed to himself. At last he knew the secret, and he decided to pay a visit of his own to the robbers' den soon. Then he would be the richest man in the village again.

He had horses harnessed to a carriage and set off at once. When he came to the foot of the mountain he recited the magic spell. The rock opened up and he went in, and almost fainted away when he saw all the riches displayed before him. He stuffed his pockets with silver and gold, and then picked up handfuls of jewels and put them in a big sack. At last he decided it was time to get away with his loot. But then he found that he couldn't remember what he must say to make the rock open and let him out of the cave.

"Mount Simeli, open up!" he said. "Mount Simeli, open up!"

But that was not the mountain's name, and the rock remained deaf to his cries and would not open.

Hours passed by, and the unhappy man ran around in circles among the treasures that were no use to him now, at his wits' end. In vain he tried to remember the right words to make the rock open. He thought so hard that his head hurt. But nothing did any good, for his memory had completely deserted him.

"Mount Simson, beautiful mountain, have mercy, let me out! Mount Somson, I'll be a good brother from now on, I'll do good in the village and I won't beat my wife and the maidservants any more!" he begged.

However, the rock remained deaf to his pleas and promises, and would not budge.

At last, some time later in the night, he heard the sound of a very loud voice outside. "Mount Semsi, open up!" it called. "Mount Semsi, open up!"

And finally the rock opened, but to the rich brother's horror twelve grim robbers came in and crowded around him. They threatened him with their guns and shouted, "You wretched thief, you've plundered our treasures several times already. Now we're going to hold you prisoner here, and you can keep strict accounts of our loot. You must make lists

of everything in this cave, and whenever we bring something new back you must write it all down."

So the rich farmer never returned to the village. His brother could guess what had happened. He took his brother's wife and her children into his own house, and looked after both the farms. And his elder brother's wife and children were happy, for now there was no one to beat them, and they led a much better life with the younger brother than they had led before.

So they all lived together for a long, long time: the farmer and the women and children were very happy, and the rich elder brother, held prisoner in the cave, was very unhappy indeed.

The Brave Little Tailor

One fine summer morning a little tailor was sitting on his table in the window, busily sewing away, just as he always did. Everyone in the town where he lived knew he was a good, hard-working tailor who always did his best, and indeed he could sew very well, and never charged a very high price.

The little tailor used to begin work early in the morning every day. As soon as the birds started to sing he woke up, rubbed his hands and said, "Now, what am I going to make today? Will it be a fine coat, or a nice pair of breeches?"

Then he would get up, eat his bread and butter and drink a mug of milk, and go to sit on his table and sew. He used to sit right in front of the window, so that whenever anything happened outside he saw it all. And every morning he greeted passers by with a cheerful "Good day to you!"

Early on this summer morning a farmer's wife went walking down the street calling, "Good jam for sale! Good jam for sale!"

That was music to the little tailor's ears. He felt a great appetite for a nice slice of bread and jam, so he put his head out of the window and

called, "Come up here, good woman, and you can sell your wares!"

The woman went up the steps to the tailor's house with her heavy basket full of pots of jam on her head, and he made her unpack them all. He looked at every one of them, picked them up, sniffed them, and finally he said, "I like good jam. You can weigh me out four ounces, my good woman, and if it comes to quarter of a pound that's all the same to me! After all, I don't buy good jam every day, so I might as well have the best there is."

The farmer's wife had hoped to sell rather more than that to the little tailor. Sighing, she weighed him out four ounces of jam, and put all the pots away again in her large, heavy basket. "You're certainly no spendthrift," said she. "You'll have finished four ounces of jam before you know it, and when you want more, just call me in again." And she went down the steps with the heavy basket on her head and walked away quickly.

"This is excellent jam," said the little tailor to himself. "It will do me good and make me strong." So he took a loaf out of the cupboard, cut off a good slice and spread it with jam. "That looks delicious," said he, "but I must finish this jacket before I get my teeth into it."

He put the bread and jam down beside him and went on working, but he was looking forward to the bread and jam so much that his stitches became bigger and bigger, because he was trying to put the jacket together as fast as possible. Meanwhile the slice of bread and jam was waiting. The jam smelled delicious, and the smell was so strong that it wasn't long before all the flies around the place caught its scent too. A whole swarm of them came buzzing up, flew in a circle above the table, and then settled on the jam in a black heap.

"Here, who invited you? Get away from here – that bread's mine, and so is the jam. It's all for me!" shouted the tailor, shooing his unwelcome guests away. But the flies, who didn't understand human language, were not so easily dismissed, and even more of them came back. In the end the tailor lost his temper, and picking up a duster he cried, "You watch out, I'll show you! You don't think I'm going to let you eat my good jam, do you? Are you out of your minds?" And he flapped the duster at them very hard.

When he looked, he saw seven flies lying dead on his table. "My word, I'm a strong fellow!" he said, feeling rather proud of his own skill and strength. "The whole town must know of this!" he decided.

He quickly took a fine piece of leather lying on his table, cut himself out a belt, and embroidered on it, in large letters, the words: "Seven at one blow!"

"The whole town, did I say?" he added. "No, the whole world must know of this!" And his heart jumped for joy. He would never have thought he was so strong! He felt really proud of himself.

The little tailor fastened the belt around his waist and decided to go out into the world. His workshop was much too small a place for such a brave fellow as he was. Before he left, he looked around his house for anything useful to take with him. He made himself a nice jam sandwich, but apart from that he could see nothing but an old cheese, so he put the cheese in his pocket.

Out by the gate he saw a bird entangled in the bushes, chirping for help, with a big ginger cat staring greedily at it. However, the bird's wings were caught and it couldn't fly away. The little tailor freed the bird and put it in his pocket along with the cheese. Then he went swiftly on his way, and because he was nimble on his feet and not very fat, he didn't tire easily.

The road he took led him to a mountain, and when he had reached the top of the mountain the little tailor found a giant there, looking cheerfully around. He went boldly up to the giant and spoke to him.

"Good day, comrade," said he. "Are you sitting there to look at the wide world? I'm going into the world myself to seek my fortune. Do you fancy coming with me?"

The giant stretched, looked scornfully at the little tailor and said, "Why, you imp, you're only a little dwarf!"

"That may be so," said the little tailor, as he undid his jacket to show the giant his belt with the writing on it. "But read this and you'll see what kind of a man I am."

The giant read: "Seven at a blow!", and he thought that meant the tailor had killed seven men. Seven at a blow ... he'd never have thought it of such a little midget!

He felt rather more respect for the little fellow, and decided to put him to the test. Picking up a rock, he squeezed it so hard that water trickled out, dripping to the ground in a little stream.

"Do that too," said the giant, "at least, if you're strong enough."

"Is that all?" asked the little tailor. "Why, it's an easy trick!"

And he put his hand in his pocket and brought out the cheese, squeezing it until the whey ran. "I think we're quits," he said.

The giant did not know what to make of this: how could such a small man be so strong? The little fellow was far more powerful than he had ever thought. Then the giant picked up a rock and threw it in the air, so high that it could hardly be seen with the naked eye. "Very well, dwarf, do that too if you can!" he said.

"Well thrown!" said the tailor. "But the rock must have fallen to the ground again somewhere. Now, watch me throw one up, and watch carefully, for it will never come down again."

So saying, he put his hand in his pocket, brought out the bird and threw it into the air. Delighted to be free again, the bird flew swiftly away and was never seen again.

"What do you think of that, comrade?" asked the tailor.

The giant could hardly believe his eyes. How had the little man done that trick? "You can certainly throw well, but now let's see if you can carry a load," he said. He led the little tailor to a huge, heavy oak tree lying on the ground. It had recently been struck by lightning in a thunderstorm and had fallen with a great crash.

"Help me to carry this tree out of the forest, if you're strong enough," said the giant.

"Willingly," said the little man. "You put the trunk on your shoulders and I'll hold the branches. They're sure to be the heaviest part, for a tree has many branches but only one trunk."

The giant thought that must be true, and he put the trunk over his shoulder. The tailor just perched on one of the branches, and as the giant couldn't see behind him, he had to carry the whole tree by himself, with the little tailor on it too. The tailor was very comfortable up in the branches, and he whistled the tune which goes, "Three tailors went riding right out of the town," as if carrying a tree were no trouble to him at all.

When the giant had carried the tree some way, he could go no further, and called out, "Watch out, I'm dropping the tree!"

The tailor jumped nimbly down and put both arms around the tree as if he had been carrying it all the time. "Well, you may be a great big fellow," he said scornfully, "but a tree is too heavy for you to carry! I'm disappointed in you!"

After a while they went on until they came to a cherry tree. The giant took hold of the top branches where the cherries ripened first, bent them far enough down for the tailor to reach them and told him to eat some cherries. However, the little tailor wasn't strong enough to hold the branches down, and when the giant let go they sprang back, taking the little tailor up into the air with them.

When he had come down to the ground again, unhurt, the giant said, "What's the matter? Can't you even hold those thin little branches down?"

"Oh, I'm not short of strength," replied the little tailor. "Surely you don't think holding down those branches would be too difficult for a man who's killed seven at a blow? I jumped over the tree because there were some huntsmen shooting in the undergrowth, that's all. Jump over the tree after me if you can."

The giant tried, but he couldn't jump over the tree and was stuck in the branches. So the little tailor had the better of him again.

"Seeing that you're such a brave fellow," said the giant, "you can come home with me to our cave and spend the night with us."

The little tailor agreed, and went with him. When they reached the cave they found several other giants sitting by a fire, each holding a whole

roast sheep and eating it. The little tailor looked around him and thought: there's far more room here than in my workshop at home. These giants live very comfortably.

The giant showed him a bed, telling him to lie down and get some rest. But the bed was much too big for the little tailor, and he thought he would rather have somewhere cosier where he could keep nice and warm, so he didn't lie down in the huge bed but crept into a corner. At midnight, when the giant thought the little tailor must fast asleep, he got up, took a heavy oaken club, and gave the bed a mighty blow with it. He thought he had made an end of that impudent little grasshopper, for after such a heavy blow the little tailor wouldn't live to tell his tale.

Early in the morning the giants went out into the forest, with never a thought for the little tailor, until all of a sudden he stood before them, alive and well. The giants were terrified. Expecting him to kill them all, they ran away as fast as their legs would carry them. They ran and ran until they could go no further, but by then they had crossed the border into another country, and they were so scared that they decided to stay where they were and never go back again.

The little tailor went on his way once more, following his nose. When he had been walking for a long time he came to a fine palace where a powerful king lived.

He lay down in the grass beside the gateway, and he was so tired that he fell asleep at once. As he lay there, some people came along, looked at him from all sides, and read the words on his handsome leather belt: "Seven at a blow."

"What a pity such a brave soldier has arrived in our country in peacetime!" they said. "He must be a very mighty man! We're often at war with other countries, and this great warrior could be a great help to us at such a time. It's a shame we're not fighting anyone just now!"

The little tailor heard none of this, for he was sleeping peacefully and dreaming of bread and jam, heavy trees that he could carry easily, and huge, fierce giants whom he could vanquish with a single blow. He felt so proud of his own strength that he smiled in his sleep.

Meanwhile, the people who had found him went to the king and told him what they had seen. If war were to break out, they said, this sleeping warrior would come in very useful, and he ought not to be allowed to leave at any price, for you didn't come across such a good soldier every day.

The king thought what they said was good advice, and he sent one of his servants to wait for the little tailor to wake up and then offer him a commission in the royal army. The messenger waited patiently until the tailor had slept enough to open an eye, and as he stretched comfortably the royal servant delivered his message.

The little tailor thought this an excellent way to wake up. He just dropped off to sleep, and when he woke he had a commission in the king's army! What could be better?

"That's the very reason I came here," he said. "I'm willing to serve the king!"

That same day the king welcomed him with great ceremony, he was given a grand house of his own, and from then on he was one of the most important officers in the royal army.

The king was pleased to have the little tailor's services, the tailor himself was pleased, but the other army officers were by no means so happy about the newcomer. "What can we do?" they said to each other. "If we pick a quarrel with him and he begins fighting, he'll kill seven of us at a blow. None of us will be able to stand up to him."

So they came to a decision and went to the king to resign from the army. "We don't like the idea of arguing with a man who kills seven at a blow," they said.

The king was very sorry to think of losing so many faithful servants just for the sake of one man. He wished he had never set eyes on the little tailor, and would have been only too glad to be rid of him again. But he

dared not dismiss him, for he was afraid the tailor might kill him in order to seize the throne for himself. He thought it over for a long, long time, and at last he had a plan. He sent for the little tailor and told him that as he was such a brave soldier he, the king, was going to make him an offer.

Now there were two giants living in a great, wild forest in the kingdom, and these giants did nothing but rob, murder and burn. No one could go near them, for all the people in the land were terrified of the giants.

Well, said the king, if the tailor defeated those two giants he could marry the king's only daughter, and have half the kingdom as her dowry into the bargain. In addition, he could take a hundred mounted soldiers to go with him and help him fight the giants.

"I like the sound of that," replied the little tailor. "I don't get the offer of a beautiful princess and half a kingdom every day of the week. Besides, two giants won't give me any trouble! After all, I can kill seven at one blow!"

So he willingly agreed to the king's request, and promised to get rid of the giants, even without the aid of the hundred mounted soldiers. Did

the king think a man who could kill seven at a blow would be afraid of a mere two?

The little tailor set off, accompanied by a hundred soldiers on horseback, but when he came to the outskirts of the forest where the giants lived he told the soldiers, "You just wait here. I'll deal with the giants on my own."

Then he disappeared into the forest. He looked to right and to left of him, and soon he saw the two giants lying under a tree. They were fast asleep, snoring so hard that it made the branches of the tree shake. They did not look particularly pleasant. Even when they were asleep, you could see at once that they must be terrible rogues. No wonder everyone in the country was so frightened of them!

The little tailor, never at a loss, filled his pockets with pebbles and climbed the tree. Halfway up the trunk he climbed out on a branch above the sleeping giants, and one by one he dropped his pebbles on one of the pair.

It was some time before the giant noticed anything, but then he woke

up, poked the other giant in the ribs and said, "What are you hitting me for? I didn't do anything to you!"

"You're dreaming," said the other giant. "I'm not hitting you." So they went to sleep again, and the tailor began dropping pebbles on the second giant.

"Here, what's the idea?" said the second giant. "Why are you throwing things at me?"

"I'm not throwing anything at you!" said the first giant angrily, for he was cross at being woken. They went on arguing for a while, but as they were so sleepy they decided not to discuss it any longer, and they went back to sleep.

The little tailor began his game again. He found his biggest pebble and threw it at the first giant as hard as he could.

"This is too bad!" shouted the giant. He jumped up like a madman and pushed the other giant back against a tree, so hard that the trunk trembled. But the other giant wasn't putting up with that, and he hit back as hard as he could. They both fell into such a rage that they started tearing up trees, roots and all, and battering each other with them until at last they both fell down dead.

Then the little tailor emerged from his hiding place and came into view.

"What luck they didn't tear up the tree where I was sitting, or I'd have had to jump to another like a squirrel!" he said, brushing bits of twig off his clothes.

He drew his sword and stabbed both giants through the chest a couple of times. Then he went back to the soldiers.

"The job's done," he said. "I've dealt with them both, but it was hard work. In their terror the giants tore up trees, roots and all, to defend themselves. However, what could they do against a man like me who can kill seven at a blow?"

"Aren't you wounded?" asked one of the soldiers.

"There was no danger of that," said the little tailor. "They couldn't so much as scratch me. I easily mastered the pair of them!"

The soldiers didn't believe him, and they rode into the forest to see for themselves. Sure enough, they found the giants lying on the ground surrounded by a great pile of uprooted trees and broken branches.

The little tailor went to the king for his reward. However, by now the king regretted what he had said, and he thought of a way to avoid giving the little tailor what he had promised.

"Before I give you my daughter and half my kingdom," he said, "you must perform another brave deed for me. There's a unicorn in the

forest, running wild and doing great damage. You must catch me that unicorn."

"I'm no more frightened of a unicorn than of two giants," said the little tailor. "Seven at a blow, that's my motto."

So he took a rope and a hatchet with him, went out into the forest and told the soldiers to wait for him on the outskirts of the woods. He didn't have to go far into the forest, for he soon saw the unicorn. It immediately went on the attack, and charged straight at the tailor trying to impale him on its horn.

"Calm down, calm down!" said the tailor. "Not so fast!"

He stood and waited until the creature was very close, and then he nimbly jumped behind a tree. The unicorn ran into the tree, driving its horn so far into the trunk that it couldn't get it out again, and so it was caught.

"I have you now, you stupid creature! You'd have done better not to charge at a brave man who can kill seven at a blow," said the tailor, coming out from behind the tree. He put the rope around the unicorn's neck and hacked its horn out of the tree with his hatchet. When that was done, he took the animal by the rope and led it to the king.

However, the king still didn't want to give him the reward he had earned. He had a third task. Before the tailor married his daughter, said the king, he must catch a wild boar that was roaming the woods and laying them waste, and the huntsmen could help him.

"Easy!" said the tailor. "It'll be child's play to me. I'll do it!"

He did not take the huntsmen to the forest with him, and they were more than glad of that, for they had met the wild boar several times before, and only just escaped in time, so they never wanted to set eyes on the creature again.

When the boar saw the tailor it made for him, foaming at the mouth and baring its tusks, and tried to knock him down. But the clever little tailor quickly ran into a chapel that stood nearby. Then he immediately jumped through a window and out again. The wild boar chased in after the little tailor, but he had quickly run around outside and slammed the door behind the boar. Now the wild beast was trapped, for it was much too fat and clumsy to jump out of the window itself. It stormed around its narrow prison, but that was no good: it was caught and it could not escape, and the little tailor called the huntsmen to come and see for themselves that he had captured the boar.

This time the king had to keep his promise, although he did not do so gladly. He gave the tailor his daughter and half his kingdom. If he had known it was no strong and mighty warrior but only a little tailor standing before him, he would have been even sorrier.

The wedding was held with great pomp and magnificence, but no one was really happy. The king did not like having given away his daughter as a reward to a soldier, a man of whom he was afraid, and the princess didn't like her new husband much either. However, the tailor became king of half the kingdom.

Some time later the young queen heard her husband talking in his sleep. "Boy," he murmured, "finish sewing me that jacket at once, and mend me those breeches, or I'll break my yardstick over your head!"

Now the queen knew her husband's secret, and realized that she had married a tailor instead of a brave soldier. The next day she went straight to the old king her father to complain. A princess can't be married to a little tailor, and she begged her father to get rid of him.

The king said he would, and told her, "Leave your bedroom door open tonight. My servants will keep watch, and when he's asleep they will come in and bind him hand and foot. Then they'll take him away and put him aboard a ship bound for the end of the world."

The queen was satisfied with that, but the young king's squire, who had overheard the whole plot, did not like it, and gave it away to his master.

The tailor listened carefully. It did not surprise him at all that his wife and her father had thought of such an underhand plan, for he had realized long before now that they did not like him.

"I'll soon deal with this," he said, for he knew at once what to do.

That evening he went to bed with his wife, just as usual. When she thought he was asleep she rose, opened the door, and went back to her bed again.

But the little tailor, who was only pretending to be asleep, began calling out in a loud voice, "Boy, sew me that jacket and mend me those breeches or I'll break my yardstick over your head! I've not only slain seven at one blow, but I've killed two giants, I've captured a unicorn and a wild boar, and do you really think I'm afraid of the men standing outside my bedroom door?"

When the king's servants heard the tailor say this they were frightened to death, and they ran away as if the devil were on their heels. After what the little tailor had said in his sleep, none of them ever dared come near him again.

Little Brother and Little Sister

Once upon a time there was a man who had two children, a son and a daughter. He and his wife loved the children dearly, and the four of them were very happy together. But it was not to last, for one sad day the children's mother fell sick, so sick that on an even sadder day she died.

The little boy and the little girl were very unhappy, and so was their father. The little house seemed so quiet! But there was an end to that, for a year later the father married again.

The children did not like their new stepmother. She was never kind to them, and she often beat them. They had only to do something their stepmother did not like, and they would both get a sound thrashing from her, and because she was afraid she might not hit them hard enough, she beat them with a stick.

One day, when the boy and the girl were older, Little Brother said to his Little Sister, "We can't go on like this. We've been so unhappy since our

mother died, and I can't bear it any more. I'd rather run away."

"You're right," said Little Sister. "Our stepmother is just like a witch."

So the boy and the girl decided that they really would run away, because they could stand their treatment no longer: They were tired of being beaten so hard and given so little to eat every day. Why, even the dog led a better life than they did!

In the middle of the night they set off.

"Where are we going?" asked Little Sister.

"I don't know," said Little Brother, "but that doesn't matter so long as we get away." And they began walking in the direction of the distant mountains.

They walked on without stopping for several hours, and as day began to dawn, Little Brother said, "Let's sleep now, and then we can go on again later." And so they did.

They slept by the roadside until afternoon. Then Little Sister opened her eyes and said, "We must go on now!"

It was very hot, and the sun stood high in the sky. Its rays beat down, so that the two children soon began to perspire. They walked over the moors, along narrow little paths through the meadows and over little bridges, and at the end of the day they came to the foot of the mountains.

However, they did not know that their stepmother was following them. She kept walking behind the children, keeping her distance from them, for something else the children did not know was that their stepmother really was a witch. They knew she was cruel, but they never guessed that she could work magic.

"Oh, I'm so thirsty," said Little Brother. "I must drink from the very first stream we come to."

Hand in hand, the two children went in search of water. They walked through the trees and had to climb some way uphill before they saw a clear little mountain stream at last.

"Don't drink!" said Little Sister to her Little Brother "Don't drink! I can hear what the stream is whispering. It says: 'If you drink from me, a tiger you will be!' This must be our stepmother's doing."

Little Brother was parched with thirst, but he didn't drink. They went on, looking for another stream.

After a while they came to another stream of water, and the boy was about to take his first sip when Little Sister cried out, "Stop! Don't drink! Listen to the water! It's murmuring: 'If you drink from me, a wolf you will be!' If you drink the water of this stream you will become a wild beast and tear me to pieces!"

"If you say so, I won't drink," said Little Brother. "But I must drink from the next stream we find, come what may!"

They went on, and at last they came to a third stream, and the water here was whispering. "If you drink from me, a deer you will be!"

"Don't drink, Little Brother!" cried the girl, but it was too late. The boy was so thirsty that he drank and drank, and immediately he turned into a deer.

Little Sister began to weep. She put her arms around the deer who was really her brother. "Oh, Little Brother," she said, "please don't leave me alone. I'm so frightened!" And the deer wept too, and promised to stay with her always.

So the deer and the girl went on, until late that evening they came to a little house. It was empty, and they decided to stay there.

The little girl found an old basket in the house, went into the woods and gathered a great heap of moss to make a bed for the deer, as well as an armful of tender grass for her brother to eat.

The deer was very happy. He ran around the forest all day, or went out walking with Little Sister. Their little house was comfortable, neat and tidy, and there was even a real stove to warm it in cold weather. Indeed, the little deer and the girl had been very lucky. The only thing wrong was that they could not break the magic spell on Little Brother.

One day the king of the country where Little Brother and Little Sister were living held a great hunt for guests from another land, as he did every year. Mounted on swift horses, they set out to catch game in the forest. In their little house, the deer and the girl heard the sound of hunting horns. "Oh, I must go and see the hunt!" cried the deer when he heard the noise. "I must be there!"

"But why do you want to go?" asked the girl. "You will be chased and caught, and then I'll have no Little Brother any more!" However, the little deer insisted on going out to see the hunt, and in the end his Little Sister had to let him go.

Before the deer went away, she said, "Remember that you must come back before dark. Knock on the door and say: 'Dear Little Sister, let me in.' If you don't say those words exactly, I won't open the door to you." Little Brother promised to do as she said, and ran out of the house to where he heard the sound of hunting horns.

The king saw the fine deer, and he gave chase at once, galloping after the animal on his horse. His hound ran beside him to catch the deer. The king spurred on his horse, but the deer always kept ahead of him, running faster and faster. A count and a baron joined the chase and went after the deer as well, yet still the animal was too fast for them.

"I have him, I have him!" cried the king when he was almost about to bring down the deer. But the deer leaped to the right and escaped the king's hound just in the nick of time. All day the deer ran on ahead of his pursuers, always keeping in front of them.

In the evening the king and the counts and barons went back to the castle, where they had a banquet with a great deal to eat, and plenty of wine. As for the little deer, he returned to the house in the forest.

"Dear Little Sister, let me in!" he called after tapping on the door with one hoof, and immediately his sister opened the door.

"Oh, I was so afraid they had caught you!" said Little Sister. "You must never, never go away again!"

Next morning the deer woke feeling cheerful. What a fine day he had spent yesterday! Once again Little Brother wanted to join the hunt, and what was that he heard? The sound of horns in the distance, blowing: "Tantantara!" There was to be another hunt!

"I want to go out! The hunt is calling me!" he told his sister.

"Oh, stay at home, Little Brother!" the girl said to the deer. "I am sure you won't come back alive today."

Whatever she said, however, the deer wanted to go out, and at last his sister let him go. "But remember to say just what I told you yesterday," she said, "or I won't let you in."

And the deer promised. He ran off in the direction of the sound of the horns, and a little later he saw the first horse, with a stout count riding it. A barking hound gave chase to the deer, and at once he turned and began to run.

Three huntsmen came up and pursued him for a long time. They had two fast hounds with them to help them catch the deer, but it was all in vain.

The deer kept ahead of them, enjoying himself, for he thought it wonderful to run for his life and outstrip all the counts and barons, even the king himself!

As evening came on and dusk was falling, the deer was hemmed in by the three huntsmen and their two hounds. They almost caught him, but then the deer suddenly turned another way and escaped. However, one of the hounds was quick enough to bite one of his hind feet.

It hurt, and the little deer was limping slightly as he ran away. Of course he was not so fast as before, with his injured foot, and one of the huntsmen had time to see that the deer wore a golden collar around his neck.

This must be a special kind of animal, he thought, and surely there's something very strange about it, for what wild deer wears a golden collar? So the huntsman followed the deer all evening until he came to the little house in the forest. Then he saw the deer tap at the door and

say, "Dear Little Sister, let me in." And he saw the girl open the door at once to let the animal in.

The huntsman who had kept close on the track of the deer went straight to the king.

"Sir, I have something to tell you," he began, and the king, who felt a great interest in the deer, was enthralled by what the man had to tell him. He decided to follow the deer himself next day.

"Tantantara!" went the hunting horns next morning, the third day of the king's hunt. The little deer woke up on his bed of moss and stood by the door, stamping with impatience while his sister begged, "Oh, don't go out! Yesterday you promised you wouldn't." But whatever she said the little deer insisted on going out again, and his sister had to open the door for him. The deer's foot was healed, and he ran faster than ever before.

The king was waiting near the little house, and went after the deer on his horse. All day he hunted the animal again, and once again the deer was too fast for him.

When the hunt was almost over the king went to the house where the deer and the girl lived. The deer never noticed, for he was still fleeing from the other huntsmen as fast as he could go.

The king dismounted from his horse, went to the door of the house and knocked softly. "Dear Little Sister, let me in!" he said.

At once the door opened. The girl was very frightened when she suddenly saw a young man in an ermine cloak standing there instead of her brother.

"I am the king," said the young man, "and I want to marry you. I love you, for I never saw a more beautiful girl before! Come with me and be my queen."

Well, the girl was happy to do as the king asked, for she liked him at once, but she made one condition. "I will marry you only if my brother may come and live in the palace too." And no sooner did she say that than the deer joined them.

"I am her brother," said the deer. "Our stepmother cast a spell on me when we ran away from home." And he told the king the whole story: how they had been ill-treated at home, how the witch had poisoned the streams, and how they came to live in their little house.

The king listened to it all, and finally he said, "Come back to my palace with me. The deer can run in the palace grounds, and sleep on fresh moss in a great room when the weather is cold, and you will be queen, dear girl."

And it happened just as he said: next day the king and the girl were married in the great hall of the palace. Hundreds of barons and counts were there to wish the couple well. They were all surprised to see the deer they had been hunting, and it was hard to believe that he was the new queen's brother.

Now the wicked stepmother did not like this at all. She heard that the king was married to a beautiful girl who had been living in the forest with a deer, and she knew at once what had happened. She had expected the deer to be caught by huntsmen long ago, and the girl to have been torn to pieces by wild beasts, so she would have no more trouble from the tiresome children.
When she heard that brother and sister were well, she was very angry, so angry that she went scarlet in the face. She moaned and complained and decided to do them some harm.
Now the witch had a daughter herself, an ugly girl who was covered with spots: on her ears, on her chin, even on her toes. She was really ugly, and she was very envious of her stepsister too.
"Why is she queen, while I'm nobody?" she kept asking.
"Your time will come," said the witch.

One fine day a little prince was born in the king's palace, a sweet, lovely little baby who looked just like his mother. The whole court was delighted, and everyone congratulated the young queen.

The only person who was not happy for the young mother was the wicked witch, and she had thought of an evil plan. She went to the palace where the king and queen lived, taking her daughter. It was a long way to go, but she did not mind that.

After a few days' journey the two of them came to the palace, and the witch quickly turned her daughter into a cat and herself into a chambermaid, dressed exactly as a chambermaid in a palace ought to be dressed.

She went into the palace and up the stairs to the queen's bedroom, and the cat went after her. No one who saw her thought it odd, for she had disguised herself well.

Then she took a flask with a green potion in it out of her bag. She cast a spell to make a tea tray appear, and put a little of the potion into the cup. After that she knocked on the door and said, "Your tea is ready, Queen," and the queen said she could come in.

The queen was feeling thirsty, so she took the cup of tea the chambermaid offered her, sipped from it, and at once she fell down dead: the potion had done its work.

The witch said a magic spell, and there was her daughter again, still covered with spots from her ears to her toes.

"Put on a nightdress and a nightcap and lie down in the bed," she said to her daughter, and the ugly girl did as she was told. Soon she was lying in the big four-poster bed, looking like the queen.

That evening the king came home. He had been away to another country, and had heard of his baby son's birth only the day before, so he had been riding all night and all day to reach home as soon as he could.

The king knocked on the door, and the witch opened it just a crack and told him, "You can't come in yet. The queen is still much too weak. You can see her tomorrow." So the king did not insist, and went to bed.

At night the whole palace was asleep except for one person, and that was the nursemaid who was to watch over the child. She sat by the baby, rocking the cradle back and forth. All of a sudden she saw the real queen, but how strange she looked, as if you could see right through her! The queen went to the cradle and lifted out her child. She hugged

the baby, gave him milk to drink, and arranged the bedclothes in the cradle. Then she put him back and said:

How is my little son? How is my brother dear?
I'll come twice more, and then
I'll never come back here.

When she had said that the queen disappeared.

The nurse could not understand it, for there were guards at the door. Had they seen nothing? And why did the queen say such strange things, and look so strange herself?

Next morning she asked the guards if they had seen anyone. "No, not a soul," they said.

The nurse decided to go to the king, and told him what she had seen.

"Someone must be pretending to be the queen!" cried the king. "There's no other explanation. I will keep watch by the baby's cradle myself tonight."

And early that evening the king went to sit by his baby son's cradle, hoping he would not fall asleep. But he didn't, for as soon he sat down by the cradle the queen appeared. She gave the baby milk to drink, and made his cradle comfortable again, and then she said:

How is my little son? How is my brother dear?
I'll come once more, and then
I'll never come back here.

And once again she disappeared. The king burst out into tears, and decided to keep watch by the baby himself again the next night.

Sure enough, the following evening there he was, even earlier than the night before, and this time he had longer to wait. The queen did not appear at one o'clock, or two o'clock, or three o'clock, and the king was beginning to feel anxious.

At last, at four o'clock, the queen appeared. She went over to the cradle and stood looking at her baby.

All was perfectly still in the nursery, and not a breath was to be heard, for the king was holding his own breath and the queen wasn't breathing at all.

The queen held her child in her arms and gave him milk to drink. Then she shook out his pillow and put him back in the cradle, carefully putting the blanket over him again. She stepped back and said sadly:

How is my little son? How is my brother dear?
Alas, alas, for now
I never can come here!

Then the king rose to his feet and cried out, "Don't go away! You are my wife, and dearer to me than anyone in the world!"
Suddenly there was a bright light in the room, and the queen came back to life, breathing again. She ran to the king, flew into his arms and kissed him, and then, weeping for joy, she told him what the witch had done to her and her son.
Next day the witch and her daughter were condemned to death, and the sentence was carried out at once, for the king did not feel like waiting. At the very moment when the witch died everyone heard a sudden cry, and who should come running in from the palace garden but a young man no one had ever seen!
However, someone did know the young man, and that was the queen, for he was her brother. Now that the wicked witch was dead the spell was broken. So the king and queen could live in the palace with their son and the queen's brother, and they all lived happily ever after.

Mother Holle

Long ago there was a widow who had two daughters, or rather, she really had just one, for the other girl was her late husband's daughter. He had been her second husband, and after the death of the girl's mother, which made him very sad, he married again. In fact he married his second wife only because he thought his little daughter needed a mother, and all went well at first, but the longer they were married the worse the woman treated her stepdaughter. After a while the girl's father died of grief, for it was all too much for him; not only did he miss his first wife, who had been much kinder than his second, but he could not bear seeing his daughter ill-treated, for he loved her better than anyone in the world.

The second wife's daughter, her child from her own first marriage, was ugly and lazy, but her mother thought far more of her than she did of the other girl. She treated her stepdaughter worse than ever after the death of her second husband, since now there was no one to keep her bad temper in check.

The girl was beautiful and kind-hearted, and was always trying to please her stepmother, but she got nothing but cross words, and she was made to work the whole time. She worked without complaining, but she received more blows than food. At times she thought she could bear it no longer, and then she would sit with tears in her eyes, thinking of her father and her real mother. However, she could not sit idle for long, for her stepmother would soon come looking for her to give her some hard, unpleasant job to do, because her lazy stepsister couldn't be bothered with it. As soon as she opened her eyes in the morning she was put to work: she had to do all the housework, weed the garden, do the washing, mend and knit, cook the meals, and see to everything else about the house.

As for her stepsister, she never lifted a finger to help, not she! She was just as quick to scold and give her sister orders as her mother, and when the mother had nothing cross to say then the daughter would make up for it. If such a thing were possible, the poor girl's stepsister was even more unpleasant to her than her stepmother was.

As soon as she had finished the housework she was sent out of doors to spend the rest of the day spinning by the side of the well – spinning rough wool which made her fingers sore until at last they began to bleed. Her fingers hurt every day, but she never complained, and indeed complaints would have done her no good.

One day her hands were bleeding so badly that the bobbin on her spindle was all red. The girl was afraid her stepmother would see the bloodstains on the wool, and she quickly bent over the side of the well to wash the blood away. But unluckily the bobbin slipped out of her sore fingers and fell to the bottom of the deep well.

Weeping and terrified, the girl ran home and told her stepmother what had happened, begging her not to be angry, for she couldn't help it. However, the stepmother said furiously that the girl must just go and get the bobbin back again.

"You dropped it into the well," she said, "so you can fetch it out again."

In her desperation, the girl climbed on the side of the well and jumped

in, hoping with all her heart that it was not very deep, so that she could reach the bottom unharmed and stand in the water. But she was wrong. First she fell for a long, long time, because the well was very deep, and then at last she hit the water, which was cold, and she felt herself sinking down and down into it. Then she lost consciousness.

Later, she could not have said how long she had lain unconscious, but when she opened her eyes again at last she was in a beautiful meadow full of flowers, with the warm sun shining down. The girl could hardly believe her eyes: she had never seen anything so beautiful before. The countryside around her looked so pleasant, as if all the flowers growing in the grass were smiling and saying, "Welcome! It's good to have you here!"

Astonished, the girl rose to her feet and looked around. In the distance, she saw a nice little house standing at the edge of the meadow. Nothing was familiar to her, and she was sure she had never been here before. Since she wanted to know where she was, she began to walk. Someone must live in the little house, and whoever lived there could tell her more. The sun had dried her wet clothes again, and she set out for the

house in good spirits. It was some way off, but that didn't matter, for the sun was shining pleasantly, and the girl enjoyed her walk.

The first thing she saw was an oven with loaves baking inside it. "Take us out, take us out!" called the loaves. "We're done to a turn and we'll burn if we stay here any longer, and then we won't be good to eat!"

The girl did not hesitate for a moment. She picked up the long wooden shovel standing beside the oven, opened the door and took the loaves out. They had been in the oven just long enough, and they looked delicious.

Then she went on and came to a pear tree, which sighed, "Oh, please pick my pears. They're so heavy I can hardly bear their weight. My branches hurt, and even my trunk is beginning to creak. You can hear it if you listen hard. I can't stand this much longer!"

So the girl found a ladder which was lying in the grass a little way off, propped it against the trunk, and spent a good hour picking all the pears on the tree. The pears seemed to be ripe, and she put them neatly in some baskets that stood at the foot of the tree. Then she went on in the direction of the little house. It looked even nicer when she was close to it. She was about to peer in through one of the windows when a face looked out at her from inside.

The face belonged to a little old woman with such big teeth that the girl took fright and was about to run away. But the little old woman came out and said, "Don't be afraid. Just come in, and if you will help me with my work you may stay with me. You must shake out my feather bed every day, and mind you shake it well so that the feathers fly, for when the feathers fly it is snowing in the world above, and that's as it should be. But first tell me who you are, and how you came here."

So the girl told her everything that had happened, and when she had finished the old woman said, "I am Mother Holle." She gave the girl food to eat, and when the sun set they both went to bed.

Next morning the girl helped Mother Holle with the housework, and she shook the old woman's bed so hard that feathers flew through the air. At the end of the day Mother Holle nodded her head, satisfied: the girl had worked well, and Mother Holle was very pleased with her.

When the girl had spent several days with Mother Holle, she knew that she was very well off here. She was never beaten or scolded, she always had plenty to eat, and Mother Holle kept praising her for her hard work. And yet after a while she didn't feel perfectly happy. She was troubled by a feeling she herself did not understand: she wanted to go home.

She thought that was silly, for she was better off where she was. She had been very unhappy at home, yet she wanted to go back to her cruel stepmother and her stepsister, who was even worse.

One morning she plucked up her courage and told Mother Holle how she felt: she wanted to go back to her own home, where she had once been so happy with her father and her real mother.

"I can understand that, my dear child," said Mother Holle, "and as you have served me so well I will take you back myself."

She took the girl's hand, and together they went a long way through a great forest. Their path led to a great gateway.

"The world above lies beyond these heavy gates," said Mother Holle. She clapped her hands, the gates opened, and the girl went through. But just as she passed under the gateway a shower of gold fell on her and stuck to her dress and her hair, so that she looked as if she were all made of gold. The girl glanced at Mother Holle in astonishment. What was happening? "That's your reward for serving me so well and industriously," Mother Holle told her. "You may keep the gold, and from now on you need never be poor again, nor will you have to ask your stepmother for anything to eat, for now you can pay for all your food and clothes yourself."

She put her hand in her pocket, and gave the girl something else. "Here," said Mother Holle, "don't forget this." It was the bobbin the girl had dropped in the well, and it was perfectly clean again, with not a stain on it. The gates immediately swung shut, squealing and creaking, and the girl looked behind her. How strange: there was no sign of the gateway she had just passed through, and if she hadn't been covered with gold she might have thought it was all a dream.

When she looked around her, she saw her own home in the distance, and a few minutes later she was running breathlessly through the garden.

The cockerel standing on the side of the well crowed:

Cock-a-doodle-do!
I will tell you true,
Our golden girl is
home again,
Cock-a-doodle-do!

The girl's stepmother believed she was dead, drowned in the well, and deep in her heart she was glad of it. Now at least she needn't trouble about her stepdaughter any more, and she could give her own daughter all her attention. But when the girl came home all covered with gold she was even happier, for she loved money better than anything else in the world. The more money the better, she thought, and she was never satisfied.

Of course she made the girl tell her what had happened, and how she came by all that gold. Then the stepmother made her decision: her own ugly, lazy daughter must go away and come back covered with gold too. So the ugly girl was sent to the well with a skein of wool and a bobbin. Her mother pricked her finger hard with a needle to make blood drip on the bobbin, and then she threw it into the well. The ugly daughter didn't want to jump down the well at all. She was frightened of water, and thought wells were frightening. She protested as hard as she could, she wept and wailed and shouted and screamed, but it was no good. The girl's mother pushed her over the side of the well, and she disappeared under the water, just like her stepsister a few weeks earlier. And just like her stepsister, she too woke up in a beautiful meadow full of flowers. She rose to her feet, saw the little house her stepsister had described in the distance, and set off.

When she came to the oven, and heard the loaves begging her to take

them out, she snapped, "I'm not a fool. I don't want to burn my hands. You can stay where you are. Who do you think I am, pray? Hire yourselves a maidservant if you want someone to do things for you!"

When she came to the pear tree she put her hands over her eyes, swerved aside and ran past the tree, and pretended not to hear the pears asking her to pick them. She couldn't stop to do that, she thought, or she would never reach Mother Holle's house. The pear tree would just have to wait until a farmer's boy came by who was foolish enough to pick its fruit.

When the girl reached Mother Holle's little house she went straight in. She was not afraid of the old woman, but as for the girl, Mother Holle thought her even uglier than she had expected. What big teeth the child had, and what a greedy mouth, and what cunning little eyes!

For the first few days the girl spent in Mother Holle's house she willingly did everything she was asked to do. But after a while she had had enough of it – more than enough. She got up very late in the morning, and she usually forgot to shake Mother Holle's bed at all, and then no snow fell even in Siberia, where it is always cold. So everything in the world above was out of order. No snow fell, and the children couldn't ride on toboggans or make snowmen. And Mother Holle's house became dirtier and untidier all the time, for in the end the lazy girl did no housework at all.

When Mother Holle saw that, she said the girl must go home, and she would take her back to the world above herself.

The girl's eyes shone when she thought of all the gold her stepsister had brought home. At last she was going to get some gold herself, greater

wealth than she could ever make in her whole life ... and about time too, for it was very tedious here, and she didn't intend to do any nasty housework, whatever the silly old woman said!

Full of hope, she walked along the path with Mother Holle. At last the time had come! But when they reached the gateway, and the gates swung open, it was not gold that fell on the girl but a shower of pitch instead.

"That's the reward for your laziness," said Mother Holle just before the gates closed again.

So the ugly girl came home, covered with pitch, and however hard she scrubbed it and rubbed it she couldn't get it off for the rest of her life. The pitch wouldn't be shifted. Of course her mother was very angry with her and blamed her every day for being so lazy and ugly, telling her she ought to have done what her stepsister did for Mother Holle! At least her stepsister had enough gold to buy a nice little house with a garden, and would have no more cares all her life, for she had plenty of money.

And the cockerel on the edge of the well was delighted, for he had never liked the lazy girl. As soon as he saw her he began to crow as loud as he

could, so that everyone heard him, and this was what he crowed every day:

> *Cock-a-doodle-do!*
> *I will tell you true,*
> *Our dirty girl is home again,*
> *Cock-a-doodle-do!*

The Frog Prince

Long ago, in a country very far away, there lived a king who had three beautiful daughters. The youngest of the daughters was so wonderfully beautiful that when the sun shone on her face it seemed to burn more brightly than ever. The other two daughters were beautiful too, but not quite as lovely as their younger sister. With her pretty long hair, her bright blue eyes, and her skin that was softer than satin she looked just like a fairy-tale princess.

The castle where the king and his daughter lived stood in a great forest, and there was a fountain nearby. The youngest princess often went to sit beside this fountain, especially when the weather was hot. It was pleasantly cool there, with the clear water splashing up all day long. To amuse herself, she would take her ball with her. It was no ordinary rubber ball – the princess's ball was made of pure gold.

She played with it like any other child, throwing it in the air and catching it again, and of course it was rather silly of the princess to play with such a precious ball so close to the water.

And one day she had bad luck. The ball didn't drop into her raised hands, but into the water, for she had thrown it sideways instead of straight up in the air.

She immediately burst into tears, for the fountain was so deep that she knew her wonderful toy was lost for ever.

Before long she was weeping so pitifully that the leaves on the trees around the fountain rustled, the flowers closed their petals, and the water of the fountain rippled with alarm. Or no – the water was rippling not with alarm, but because a large frog put his head above the surface, paddling his webbed feet to stay in the same place, and said, "Why are you crying like that, princess? Anyone would think your palace was on fire. What's so bad that it makes you weep so miserably?"

The girl looked up and saw the frog. "Oh, it's you, is it, old croaker?" she said. "No, our palace isn't on fire, but my lovely golden ball has fallen into the water, and that's almost worse, for how will I get it back now?

Oh, it's gone for ever, and I'm so sad!" And she began crying again, even harder than before.

But the frog knew how to help her. "Well," said he, "there's no need for you to cry like that. I'm quite at home in the water, and I can bring your ball up for you. That's easy enough. What will you give me as a reward?"

"Anything you want," replied the girl. "My golden crown!"

And she took the precious crown off her head and offered it to the frog.

"What would I do with a crown?" asked the frog.

"My jewels, then, and my clothes, and my carriage with its two fine white horses."

"Oh yes, I can just imagine it!" said the frog. "A frog riding in a carriage! I don't need a carriage any more than I need your clothes. They'd just get wet. No, princess, you must think of a better reward."

"But what do you want, then?" asked the girl in despair. She had offered the frog everything she had to offer, and could think of nothing else. Was her golden ball lost for ever after all?

"I want to be your friend," said the frog. "I want you to play with me, and I want to sit next to you at table. I want to eat from a golden plate and drink from a golden goblet, just like you, and I want to sleep in your bedroom."

The princess was ready to promise anything if she could have her golden ball back, so she agreed at once, and said she and the frog would be friends for ever from now on, the very best friends in the world.

But when the frog had disappeared under the water, she thought that he was just as stupid as any other frog, for how could a frog live with human beings and be friends with them?

Almost at once the frog appeared again, and now he had the beautiful golden ball in his wide mouth. He swam to the bank and dropped the ball into the princess's outstretched hand.

The girl snatched her ball, jumped up at once and ran away. She wanted to get home as fast as she could, away from the strange frog and the deep fountain.

"Wait for me!" the frog called after her. "We're going to be friends! Come back! You promised!"

But either the princess didn't hear him or she pretended not to. Perhaps princesses are more forgetful than ordinary girls, and she had really forgotten her promise to the frog.

Next day, however, the princess had just sat down to dinner in the great banqueting hall, between her two sisters, ready to eat from her golden plate, when something came dragging itself up the marble steps, slip-slop, slip-slop! And once again it went slip-slop. It was the frog making his way up the stairs. Then he took a leap at the door of the royal banqueting hall.

He knocked on the door with one of his feet. It was only a small foot, and the door was thick and heavy, but everyone in the banqueting hall heard the knocking quite clearly, and they heard the croaking of the frog as he said, "Princess, open the door!"

Of course the princess didn't go to open the door herself, but one of the servants did, and he immediately closed it again, for he could see no one outside.

He had not looked hard enough, for the frog was sitting there all the time, and now he knocked on the door a second time and called, "Youngest princess, please open the door at once!"

The girl rose, opened the door and immediately shut it again, just as the footman had done. But she had seen who was there, calling and knocking, and the queen could tell from her face that something was the matter.

"Why are you so frightened, dear child?" she asked.

"Is it a man-eating monster at the door?" laughed the king.

"No," said the princess. "It's a frog."

"A frog!" cried her sisters in alarm.

"What does this frog want?" asked the king, while the queen began climbing on a chair. She was frightened of frogs.

Then the princess told the story of what had happened the day before: how she had let her ball fall into the water, and how she had to promise to be the frog's best friend if he brought the golden ball back to her.

"Well," said the king, "I'll eat my golden crown if I can make head or tail of this! Surely a frog can't talk. However, as you are a real princess you must keep your promise, even if it was a promise made to a frog. If you don't want to be friends with a frog you ought to have thought of it before. It's too late now. So go and let your friend in, daughter."

The princess obeyed. She went slowly to the door and opened it. The frog jumped in as quickly as he could, leaped up on the princess's chair, and then from the chair to the table. Wherever he went he left a trail of slimy footprints behind him.

When the princess was sitting down again he said, "There, now we'll eat together from your golden plate."

The princess tried to eat a morsel or two, but she didn't feel like eating any more now, with the frog right beside her, making nasty smacking noises as he ate.

The frog enjoyed his meal. He thought the royal dinner of potatoes and sprouts and almond pudding was delicious. "This is much nicer than duckweed," said he, smacking his lips when the last of it had disappeared. "Now take me to your bedroom, because it was a long way here, and after such a good meal I'd like to sleep. I'm really looking forward to sleeping in a soft, warm, royal bed."

The girl did not move, but the king looked sternly at her and said, "A princess always keeps her promises, remember."

Then the girl began to cry. "I don't want to!" she said, stamping her foot. "He's so wet and so cold and slimy and … "

"And you will do exactly as you promised," said the king. "You can't let down a person who helped you when you were in need, even if that person is only a frog," he added.

The girl picked the frog up, holding him at arm's length, and carried the creature out of the banqueting hall and to her bedroom. There she put him down on the floor in a corner and quickly got into her nightdress. Without even cleaning her teeth or brushing her beautiful fair hair, she hurried into bed under the blankets, and pulled them as close around her as possible.

But the frog was not to be put off so easily. He came hopping up and said, "I want to sleep in your bed. You promised I could, and if you don't keep your promise I'll tell your father. I did say I wanted to sleep in a nice soft bed, didn't I? Very well, move over a bit. And that's not all, because I want you to give me a goodnight kiss before I go to sleep. Friends always do that, don't they? And we are friends, aren't we?"

In her fury the princess cried and screeched so loud that her father came to see what was wrong. Weeping, she told him what the nasty frog wanted now. However, her father shook his head and said, "I can't help you, daughter. You must always keep your promises." And still shaking his head sadly, the king went away again and closed the door behind him.

Then the girl jumped angrily out of bed, closed her eyes tight and took hold of the frog. With her eyes still shut, she cautiously gave him a tiny little kiss on top of his head. But when her lips felt the frog's slimy skin it was too much for her. She wiped her mouth and, with tears in her eyes, threw the frog away from her and against the window.

She had really meant to throw him right out of the window, but she had forgotten that it wasn't open, so the frog hit the glass of the window pane so hard that he flew back in a great curve and fell to the floor.

Then a very strange thing happened. The creature didn't hit the ground with the slight sound you would expect of a frog, but with a much louder noise, and it was not a frog at all who picked himself up from the floor by the window, rubbing his sore shoulder.

Instead, there stood a young man with a very kind and handsome face, wearing fine clothes and with a golden crown on his head, just like a real prince.

At first the princess was terrified. She clapped her hand to her mouth and said nothing at all for sheer surprise. When she had finally recovered from her amazement, the handsome young man told her his story. A wicked witch had cast a spell on him, he said. She turned him into a frog and left him near the fountain in the forest. Only a real princess could free him from the enchantment, but first the princess must be willing to play with him and be friends with him, and most important of all, she must give him a kiss. The witch's spell meant that he could not be a prince again until he had eaten from the princess's place, been in her bedroom and received her kiss. That was exactly what had happened, and now the magic spell was broken for ever.

Since the girl had promised him while he was still a frog that they would

be the best friends in the world for ever, they decided to be married next day, and then the princess would go to the prince's own country as his wife.

And that was what they did. Next morning, when the princess had told her parents the whole story, and her father and mother had met the frog prince for themselves, they thought it an excellent idea for her to marry him. The wedding was held at once. Guests were quickly invited, and the wedding took place very soon. When the ceremony was over, a fine carriage drawn by six white horses came driving up the avenue leading to the palace. The princess had never seen such a beautiful carriage before. Even her father the king had no coach so fine! The doors of the carriage had golden crowns on them, and the horses' harness gleamed with gold as well.

The horses were driven by the prince's young servant, who had been deeply grieved when his master disappeared from the palace, but now he was happy again, for his master was back, and with a beautiful wife too.

So the prince and princess went to the prince's country, where they became king and queen, and they lived happily ever after.

The Griffin Bird

nce upon a time there was a king who ruled his land so well that everyone living there was very happy. However, the king was far from happy himself. For years he and the queen had longed for a child, best of all a son who could become king himself later, when the king his father grew old. But no child was born to them.

At last, when the king and queen had almost given up hope, they did have a child, a baby girl. Although the king would rather have had a son he was very happy with his daughter. However, as soon as the little girl was born they could see that her health was poor, and it was still poor years later, when she was old enough to be married. That was sad, for it meant that the king could not find any prince ready to marry his daughter. No one wanted a wife who was always sick, and whose doctors kept telling her to rest in bed.

The king had consulted doctor after doctor, but none one of them could help the girl. However, the king's own doctor assured him that the princess would be perfectly well if she ate a great many apples. The king had the finest, best and biggest apples taken to her, but although the girl ate apples from early in the morning until late at night, it was no use. She was still sick. Then the king's doctor said the apples were not good enough, so the king sent out messengers, to make it known that any man who brought him the apples that cured his daughter could marry her and be king himself one day.

The messengers rode all through the land, and so one of them came to a farmer who lived with his wife and three sons in a distant part of the country. It was always quiet there, and no one ever came by, but the king's messengers were to carry the very important announcement everywhere, even to this remote farm.

"You'd better set off at once," said the farmer to his eldest son. "The apples from our tree here are the healthiest and finest in the whole country, and if they don't help the princess then nothing can! But they will, and then you can marry her!"

210

So the young man filled a basket with beautiful, rosy apples and set off. When he had been walking for a while he suddenly saw a strange little man in front of him. "What's in your basket?" asked the little man.

"Frog-spawn," replied the young man, who thought it was none of the strange little man's business what he had with him.

"So be it," replied the little man, and he went off in the opposite direction. The young man went to the palace, where he told the gatekeeper he had brought the apples that would cure the princess.

He was let in at once, and the king came to meet him with his hand outstretched. But when the farmer's son opened his basket there were no apples in it, only frog-spawn!

The king was very disappointed, and angry too. He had the young man chased out of the palace with a whip.

Well, the farmer thought his eldest son a fool, so he sent his second son off to the palace with a basket of apples. On his way the second son too met the strange little man, who asked what he had in his basket.

"Pork," said the young man, for what business of the little man's was it?

"Well, so be it," said the little man.

The gatekeeper didn't want to let the second son into the palace at first, for he thought the young man might be an impostor, just like the other young man who had come to the gate a few days ago with a basket full of frog-spawn. But after much persuasion, the second son was let into the throne-room to open his basket in front of the king.

Sad to say, however, the basket was full of pork, and the farmer's stupid second son suffered an even worse beating than his brother before he was outside the palace gates again.

When he went home and told his story, his father could hardly believe it, but all the same he sent off his youngest son, who was known as Stupid Hans. The farmer didn't think Hans could do his errand properly, for he was so stupid that everyone around laughed at him. People even said, when someone did a silly thing, "You're as bad as Stupid Hans."

However, Hans kept pressing his father, saying he wanted to try his luck, and perhaps he thought he really might succeed and would marry a real princess.

He rose next morning before the cockerel had crowed, filled a basket with the most beautiful apples he could find, and set off. On the way he

too met with the strange little man, who stood in his path and asked what he had in his basket.

"Apples," said Hans. "The best, most beautiful apples in the whole world." At that the little man began to laugh and skip about, and he said, "Well, so be it."

Hans said goodbye to the little man and went cheerfully on. He whistled a tune as he walked and greeted everyone he met. So the time passed quickly, and he soon came to the palace gate. He had to talk to the gatekeeper for a good hour before he was let in, and once he was inside the king warned him, "If you're an impostor I'll shut you up in a dungeon underneath the palace, and you will never get out again!"

But Hans, who had packed the apples in the basket himself, after all, opened it up confidently, and the king's eyes widened with amazement when he set eyes on those splendid apples, the best he had ever seen. If these apples could not cure the princess, then she would surely be sick all her days.

The king had them taken to his daughter at once, and she immediately began eating them. Only quarter of an hour later the king's doctor came to tell him that the girl was beginning to recover, and five apples and another half an hour later she was perfectly well.

The king was very happy, so it was strange that Hans wasn't married to the princess at once. However, the king took one look at him, and he thought at the bottom of his heart that Hans seemed a little simple, and he would rather have married his daughter to a man who at least had all his wits about him. Moreover, the man who married his daughter would be king one day, and lord of the whole land. So first, the king decided, Hans must show what he was good for. He would give the lad a difficult task, and if he carried it out well then he might marry the princess at once. So he told Hans to make a ship to sail on dry land.

The young man said he would do as the king asked, and he went home and told his family what had happened. Then his father sent his eldest son to the forest to make the ship.

When the eldest son had almost finished, the strange little man appeared again, and asked what he was making.

"I'm making a barrel," replied the young man.

"Well, so be it," said the little man, and he went away.

When the eldest son thought his ship was ready, it turned out that he could do nothing with it. On land, he could move it forward only if he pushed it, and in the water it turned around like a top.

His father said the eldest son was useless, and he sent the second son out to try. While the young man was at work, the strange little man came along and asked what he was building.

"A house," said the young man.

"Well, so be it," said the little man, and he disappeared again.

That evening it looked as if the son had spoken the truth, for there stood his ship as firmly fixed to the forest floor as if it were a house, and he couldn't get it to move at all.

When he told his father, the farmer said he was good for nothing, and would never marry a princess and become king.

Then it was the turn of Stupid Hans. He went busily to work, and when the little man came to ask what he was making, he said he was building a ship that could sail on land even better than on water, and when it was made he would marry the lovely princess he had cured with his apples.

"Well, so be it," said the little man, and off he went.

By evening the ship was ready. Hans climbed aboard, hoisted the sail, and he was at the palace in no time at all.

The king had seen him coming from afar, and he was amazed that the simple farmer's boy had carried out his task so well. But still he didn't like the idea of marrying his daughter to Hans, so he thought of yet another trick.

He told Hans that he must spend a whole day, from sunrise to sunset,

herding a hundred hares, letting them run and play in the meadow and eat clover, but he must watch them well, and if a single hare was missing in the evening then he couldn't marry the king's daughter.

"Oh, none of them will run away!" Hans told the king confidently, and he went out to the meadow behind the palace with the hares.

However, the king had another trick up his sleeve. He sent the kitchen maid out to Hans to fetch a hare, saying the king of a nearby country had suddenly come on a visit, and wanted to eat jugged hare.

But Hans refused, saying that if the king needed a hare he must come for it himself, and if he wouldn't then he must just give his guest pork to eat. After all, he had a basket full of pork brought by the farmer's second son.

The kitchen maid was hardly out of sight before the strange little man appeared and asked Hans what he was doing.

"I'm herding a hundred hares," said Hans, "and if they're still all here by evening I can marry the princess."

Then the man gave him a tiny whistle. "If one of your hares runs away," he said, "just blow this whistle and it will come straight back."

A little later the king himself did indeed come to fetch a hare, and Hans willingly gave him one. The king chose the biggest, fattest hare of all and went off to the palace kitchen with it, chuckling. He had fooled the farmer's son nicely now!

However, before the king could reach the palace with the big hare, Hans blew his whistle. The hare jumped out of the king's arms and ran back to Hans.

Nothing more happened that day. Now and then Hans blew his whistle, and when he blew it all the hares came running up and let him count them. Sometimes they even sat on his lap to be petted. The king was amazed when Hans brought back all the hundred hares in the evening.

However, instead of agreeing to let his daughter marry Hans he thought of yet another task. This time, he said he wanted three tail feathers from the Griffin Bird.

Hans did not hesitate, but said he would go and get the feathers, and he set off at once. He liked the prospect of a good walk, for he enjoyed walking. On his way he greeted everyone he met in friendly tones, just as he always did.

As evening began to fall, Hans came to a great castle. He knocked at the door and asked if he might spend the night there. The knight who lived in the castle let him in, and asked where he was going. Hans told him he was off to see the Griffin Bird.

"The Griffin Bird!" said the knight. "Well, this is a lucky thing! They say he knows everything, so when you speak to him, perhaps you could ask him where I lost the key of my money-box, for I can't find it anywhere.

But you must be very careful. The Griffin Bird is a bloodthirsty monster who eats human beings. Only a little while ago he took the baby son of some friends of mine, cradle and all, and we're almost sure he ate the child. So I warn you, take care."

Hans promised he would, went to bed early, and rose early next morning to go on his way to the Griffin Bird.

That night he slept at another castle, for he could find no inn anywhere. When the people who lived in the second castle heard that Hans was on his way to the Griffin Bird, they begged him, with tears in their eyes, to ask the wise creature how they could cure their daughter, who had been sick for a very long time. Hans promised that he would, went to bed early, and set out again early the following morning too.

He had almost reached the end of his journey when all of a sudden he came to a broad river. What was he to do now? There was no boat in sight, only a ferryman who carried anyone who wanted to cross the river over it in his arms.

"When you come to the Griffin Bird," said the man, "ask him how I can be rid of this job. I have to toil away every day, carrying people over the river, and I've had enough of it. I'm drenched several times a day, and it's no kind of a life at all!"

Hans promised to ask and went cheerfully on his way. Soon he came to the Griffin Bird's house, but only the bird's wife was at home.

Hans told her why he had come: he must have three feathers from the Griffin Bird's tail, he must ask where the lord of the first castle's lost key was, and he must ask how the daughter of the people living in the second castle could be cured. Finally, the ferryman who carried people over the river wanted to know how he could be rid of his tedious job.

"Well," said the Griffin Bird's wife, "it's a good thing you found me at home on my own, for my husband would have eaten you up at once. He generally eats any human beings he can find."

"What am I to do?" asked Hans. "I can't leave without the feathers, and I don't want to fail the people who helped me on my way here."

"Just go and lie under my husband's bed," said the Griffin Bird's wife. "Then you can pull out the feathers while he's asleep, and I will ask him your questions."

"But suppose he doesn't know the answers?" asked Hans.

"My husband knows the answer to anything I ask him," said the woman.

No sooner said than done. Hans went into hiding and waited for the Griffin Bird to get into bed.

"I smell human flesh!" said the bird, sniffing, as soon as he came home. "You're quite right," said his wife. "Someone was here today, but he left." Luckily the bird was satisfied with this answer. He went to bed, closed his eyes, and soon his snoring told Hans he was fast asleep.

Hans crawled cautiously out from under the bed, gave a mighty tug, pulled out three tail feathers, and immediately got back under the bed with them. The bird woke with a loud, "Ouch!", and he rubbed his tail, looking sorry for himself.

The bird's wife heard the noise and came in. "What's the matter?" she asked.

"I smell human flesh," said the bird, "and what's more, my tail hurts!"

"I can't help it if your tail hurts, and you smell human flesh because, as I told you, someone was here this afternoon."

"What did he want?" asked the bird drowsily.

"He wanted to know where the lord of a certain castle had put the key to his money box."

"The fool!" said the bird. "It's lying under a stack of logs by the hearth."

"And the daughter of the people who live in another castle is sick and can't be cured," went on his wife.

"Well, that just shows human beings are so stupid, they're no good for anything but being eaten!" snorted the bird. "The girl is sick because a mouse has made a nest of hair stolen from her head. The nest is under the cellar stairs. If she gets her hair back she will be cured at once."

"And you know the ferryman by the river? He wants to be rid of his work, for he's had enough of carrying everyone over the river."

"Well, that's easy," said the bird, smiling. "He only has to drop the first person who comes along into the middle of the river, and he'll be rid of the job at once. Now let me sleep!"

Soon the Griffin Bird's house was echoing to the sound of his snoring. But before long, as soon as there was a little light, the bird rose and went away, and so did Hans. He had three fine feathers, and answers to all his questions.

When he came to the man who was to carry him over the river, Hans had himself taken to the opposite bank, and then answered the ferryman's question: he only had to drop the next person to come along in the

middle of the river, and then he needn't ferry people across any more. The man was very grateful, so grateful that he said he would happily carry Hans over the river once again. However, Hans refused this kind offer and went on his way cheerfully, until he came to the castle where the sick girl lived.

He told the lord of the castle and his wife what the bird had said. They began searching at once, and they very soon found the nest the mouse had made and gave their sick daughter her hair back.

That evening, when Hans went to bed, she was beginning to recover, and by the next morning she was quite better. The sick girl's parents were so happy they didn't know how to thank Hans, so they gave him a great many fine presents, and Hans went on again, taking the presents. In the other castle, he himself found the key where the Griffin Bird had said it was. Just as the bird's wife said, the Griffin Bird knew everything. How happy the knight who lived in that castle was! Now at least he could get at his money again, and the first thing he did was to take handfuls of gold pieces out of the money-box and give them all to Hans.

So laden with money, gold and jewels, Hans came back to the palace at last and gave the king the feathers he had asked for.

The king wanted to know how Hans had come by all his wealth, and Hans said the Griffin Bird had given it to him because he was a messenger from the king. He added that the Griffin Bird would very much like to meet the king himself, and would give him more and better presents than he had given Hans.

The king thought that was very kind of the Griffin Bird, and entirely forgot to hatch any more plots to keep Hans from marrying the princess. He set off at once to go and see the Griffin Bird.

When he came to the river he was the first person after Hans to ask the ferryman to carry him over to the other bank. So the ferryman dropped him in the middle of the river, and as the king couldn't swim he sank beneath the surface, floundering, and never came up again.

Hans married the princess and became king. He was such a good king that the people of that country soon forgot the old one, for they had never been ruled so well as they were ruled by Hans.

The Six Servants

Long, long ago, in the days when there were still witches, an old queen who could work magic lived in a country very far away. The king of that land was dead and gone long ago, and the queen lived alone with her daughter in the great palace.

As the old king had died, the queen ruled the country, and the people living there did not like it, for the old queen was not good to them.

Now the queen's daughter was very beautiful, so the old enchantress ought really to have been content, but she wasn't. There was only one thing she enjoyed, and that was making other folk miserable. With that in mind, she even wanted her daughter the princess to be as wicked as herself. But the princess was good and kind, and could not be like her mother. And because she was so good and kind many young men came asking for her hand in marriage. The queen would agree, and say the wedding would be held soon, but first the young man must perform a task she would set him, and if he did not succeed, he must die. However, no one could perform the difficult tasks she set. Of course this made the princess very sad, but she could do nothing about it. Whenever she tried to persuade her mother not to set a young man such a difficult task, the queen would say, "My child, I want to know if this is a good, brave man you want to marry, for your husband will be king of our land one day, so I must make sure he is clever and brave."

The girl was so good and beautiful that there were always plenty of young men coming to try their luck, but the queen set such difficult tasks that no one ever succeeded, and one by one the princess's suitors had their heads cut off.

Now the prince of a land nearby had heard of the beautiful girl, and he asked his father's consent to his marriage with her. He had to ask his father, because one day, when the king was too old to rule, the prince would be king himself.

"Never!" said his father. "It won't do, for if you try you will be set some dreadful task to perform too, and you will surely die, and then what will happen when I die myself? Don't forget that you are to rule this land one day."

Then the prince was very sad, so sad that he fell sick and had to take to his bed. He lay sick for seven long years, and no doctor could cure him. The last doctor who came to look at the prince said he was sure he would never recover.

At that his father said sadly, "Well, if no doctor can help you, then go and do as you wish."

No sooner had his father said this than the prince rose from his bed and began making ready for his journey, perfectly well again.

He set out early the next morning, and he was cheerfully crossing a great stretch of moorland when he saw something in the distance – a dune, he thought, or a high hill. But he was wrong, for as he came closer he saw that it was the stomach of someone who lay there snoring.

This person, an enormously fat man, tried to get to his feet, and he asked the prince if he happened to need a servant.

"What would I do with such a fat fellow as you?" asked the prince.

"Do you really think me too fat?" asked the man, who was known as Fatman. "You ought to see me when I really puff myself out! I'm thousands of times fatter then."

"Well, come along with me," said the prince. "If that's true, I'm sure I can use your services."

Fatman waddled along after the prince, until they saw someone lying on the grass a little further on, with his ear to the ground.

"What are you doing?" asked the prince.

"Nothing," said the man. "I'm just listening."

"What is there to hear?" asked the prince.

"I hear everything that happens in the world," said the man. "Nothing escapes me, so they call me Sharpears. I can even hear the grass growing."

"What can you hear in the palace of the queen with the good and beautiful daughter?" said the prince at once.

"I hear the swish of the sword cutting an unfortunate man's head off," said the man.

"If you will be my servant too," said the prince, "I could use your services."

The man joined them, and they went on. After a while they saw a pair of feet on the ground, and the feet were joined to legs and everything else that belongs to a man, but this man's feet and head were so far apart that the prince said, "Why, what a tall fellow you are, and how long your neck is!"

"Oh, this is nothing," said the man, who was called Lanky. "Tall? You haven't seen anything yet. If I really stretch, I'm a thousand times as tall, taller than the highest mountains on earth. I'll be a good servant to you if you can use me."

"Yes, I can," said the prince, "so come with me." And they went on again.

Next they met a man sitting by the road with a blindfold tied over his eyes. "Is the sunlight too bright for your eyes?" asked the prince.

"No, by no means," said the man. "My problem is that my eyes are much too keen. If I just look at anything, it will break into pieces, so that's why I have to wear this blindfold. If I can be of any service to you, my name is Fiery Eyes."

"Come with me," said the prince. "I'm sure you will be useful."

They went on again, until after several hours they saw a man lying on the ground in the hot sunlight, shivering with cold.

"Are you sick?" asked the prince. "Can we help you? Would you like us to take you to a hospital?"

"I don't need to go to any hospital," replied the man. "I'm perfectly well, just a little cold!"

"How can you be so cold if you're not sick?" asked the prince. "The sun is blazing down, and this is the hottest time of the day!"

"It's because I'm not like other people," said the man. "The hotter the sun, the colder I feel, and I get warmer as the weather gets colder, which is a strange thing, don't you agree?"

"You certainly are a strange fellow," said the prince, "but if you'd like to be my servant, then come along with us, and we'll call you Hot-and-Cold."

A little further on they saw a man craning his neck so far that he could see over all the mountains.

"What do you see?" asked the prince.

"Oh, everything," said the man. "I have eyes that can see through anything, and I see whatever goes on in the world. It comes in very useful. My friends call me Sharpsight."

"Then you must be my servant," said the prince. "I'm sure I can use your services."

So the prince and his six servants came to the city where the old queen lived with her lovely daughter. The prince went straight to see the old queen, but he didn't say he was a prince himself and would be a king some day, he only asked for her beautiful daughter's hand in marriage.

"And I will perform any task you set me," he promised.

The queen smiled unpleasantly. She was pleased to see another young man, and a handsome young man at that. She would set him a very difficult task, she thought, so difficult that he would never be able to perform it. And then – well, it would be hard on the handsome young man, but she would have him beheaded.

"You look a fine young fellow to me," she said in friendly tones, "and I think you'd make a good bridegroom for my daughter, but first I must see that you are worthy of a princess, so I am going to set you three tasks. If you perform them all well you may marry my daughter."

"What do you want me to do?" asked the prince.

"The first task is not very easy," said the old queen, laughing. "You must bring me back a ring I dropped in the Red Sea."

The prince nodded to show that he agreed and went back to his servants to discuss it with them. That did not take long, for Sharpsight said he would look and see just where the ring lay.

He stared into the depths of the Red Sea, and there he saw the ring, caught on a pointed rock under the water.

They all went there quickly, carried by the tall man, Lanky, who was

going to take it off the rock, but he couldn't see it, so Fatman lay flat on his stomach, and in half an hour he drank the whole sea dry. When he had finished the sea bed looked like a desert. There wasn't a drop of water left.

Then Lanky bent down, picked up the ring and gave it to the prince, who took it to the queen. The queen could hardly believe her eyes when she saw that he had succeeded in finding her ring in the great Red Sea, and had brought it back too. But she showed nothing, and gave the prince a second task.

"There are three hundred fat cows grazing in the pastures outside my castle," said the queen, "and there are three hundred barrels of wine down in my cellars. You must eat the cows, hide and hair and all, and wash them down with the wine. If there's so much as a single hair from the cows or a single drop of wine left, you must die, do you understand?"

"Of course," said the prince. "It's easy to understand, and your task doesn't seem to me too difficult. I hope the third will be a really hard

one. However, of course I will do as you ask, although I'd like to have a friend with me. I'd rather have company at table than be on my own."

"You may invite one guest," said the queen, smiling, "but only one, no more."

The prince went to his servants and asked Fatman if he would eat with him that day. Fatman puffed himself out to a thousand times his usual size, and he had plenty of room for the three hundred cows and the wine, which he drank straight from the barrels.

"Is that all?" he asked when he had finished.

"I'm afraid so," said the prince, and he went to the palace to tell the queen he had carried out her second task just as she wished: there wasn't a single hair or a single drop of wine left.

The queen was astonished to find that the prince had succeeded where everyone else had failed. "No one ever got as far as this before," she said, and in fact she was a little afraid, for suppose this strange fellow were to perform all her tasks? However, she wouldn't even think of that! And fortunately the third task was the most difficult of all. So she told the prince, "You still have one task to perform, and if you succeed, we can talk about the wedding. So listen to me, young man. I will bring my daughter to your room this evening. You may hold her in your arms, but make sure you keep awake and don't fall asleep, for if my daughter isn't in your arms when the clock strikes twelve, you are lost."

The prince thought this was not too difficult a task. I'll be sure to keep

my eyes open, he thought, if only because I'll be so glad to look at the lovely princess.

However, he summoned his servants to tell them what the queen had said, and he added, "But I think there's something behind it. I believe the wicked old queen has a cunning plan in mind. So you must keep watch, and make sure the princess doesn't leave my room."

When it was dark, the queen brought her daughter to the prince's room, and he was happy to put his arms around the beautiful girl. As for the princess, she looked at the prince, saw that he had very kind eyes, and thought there were far worse places to be than in the arms of this fine young man. Then Lanky came and coiled his great length around the prince and princess, and Fatman went and sat outside the door, so that no one could come in or go out unnoticed.

There sat the prince with the beautiful princess, who never said a word. But the moon shone in through the window, so that the prince could see just how beautiful she was. He never tired of gazing at her, and he loved her more and more all the time. He was sure he would never close his eyes!

However, the wicked queen cast a spell on them all to send them to sleep, the prince and his servants, and then the girl disappeared.

The prince and Lanky and Fatman slept for exactly an hour, and then the magic wore off.

"I am lost!" cried the prince in despair, when he saw that the princess was not in his arms any more. Fatman and Lanky wept and wailed too, for they thought a great deal of their master, and besides, they were terribly afraid that they would be beheaded as well.

However, Sharpears, who heard everything, asked them to be quiet, for he thought he could hear something, and he wanted to listen.

After a moment he said, "The princess is sitting on a rock very far away, weeping because of what has happened to her. Lanky, stand up and stretch yourself as far as you can, and if you walk at a good pace you'll soon be there."

"Very well," said Lanky, "I'll do that – I mean, I'll go there, but let Fiery Eyes go with me, for I don't want any trouble with the rock." So he picked up Fiery Eyes, who was still wearing a blindfold, put him on his shoulders and set off.

With his great long legs, Lanky took only half an hour to reach the rock. Once they were there, Fiery Eyes removed his blindfold. He just looked at the rock and at once it broke into thousands of pieces. The girl, who had been sitting on top of it, fell down along with all the chunks of rock, but Lanky easily caught her and held her in one arm, and with Fiery Eyes in his other arm he had returned to the prince within half an hour. When the clock struck twelve they were all together once more as if nothing had happened, and they were very curious to find out what the old queen would say.

In she came. You could see that she was very pleased because she thought her daughter was far, far away, sitting on a rock, and the young prince would be beheaded in the morning. And it was even clearer to see that she was furious when she saw the girl in the prince's arms.

So now the young man had performed all her tasks, she thought, and she was right. She had to agree to let him marry her daughter.

However, the wicked queen still had a plan. She swiftly whispered to her daughter that it was a shame for her to have to marry a common man, and a man with such strange servants as well, for now she could never be married to a real prince and live in a fine castle. For the wicked queen still didn't know that the young man was a real prince himself, and would be king one day.

Then the princess was angry too, because she would have liked to be married to a real prince, and so she told the young man that he had performed the three tasks her mother set, but now she would set him some tasks of her own.

She had three hundred bundles of firewood brought and built into a great bonfire, which she set alight. Then she told the prince someone must sit on top of the bonfire, or she would never be his wife.

"This is a task for you, Hot-and-Cold," said the other servants to the man who felt cold when it was hot and hot when it was cold, "and about time too, for you haven't done anything for our master yet!"

So Lanky picked Hot-and-Cold up and put him on top of the bonfire, where he stayed until all the wood was burnt and the bonfire had collapsed. Hot-and-Cold came out of the ashes with his teeth chattering, complaining, "I was never so cold in my life before. That's the first and last time I do anything of the sort. Give me the sun – it's so nice and

cool. But as for this fire, I was almost frozen! I'm numb with cold!"

The queen and her daughter were at their wits' end now, for at last the wedding must be held. So a little later a magnificent carriage with the prince and princess inside it drove to church.

Suddenly, however, the queen had another idea. She summoned her general and told him that all the soldiers in the army must go and bring her daughter back. "And anyone who fights the soldiers is to be taken prisoner," she said.

But Sharpears had heard everything: the whole plot the queen had hatched and the orders she had given her general.

"What can we do?" he asked Fatman, and Fatman thought of something at once. He had drunk up the whole Red Sea, so now he opened his mouth and let all the water of the sea out again. Soon there was a great lake in the soldiers' way, and they were all drowned.

When the queen heard of that she sent out ships with more soldiers in them, for she was determined to get her daughter back. The ships were full of armed knights who fought so well that no one could defeat them. But Sharpears heard the clinking of their coats of mail, and he took the

blindfold off Fiery Eyes, who only had to look at the ships and the coats of mail to make them fall to pieces, and without their ships and their coats of mail the knights couldn't fight.

So at last the prince and princess came to church and were married. After that the servants left. "You don't need us any more," they said, "so we will go on our way and see if anyone else can do with our services."

The prince immediately set off with his bride for his father's castle, and after a journey of several days he came to the village that lay near it. The first person he met there was the swineherd coming down the road with his pigs.

"I have something to tell you," said the prince to his bride. "I am a swineherd, and the man we saw there is my father, so now we have to go and help him look after the pigs."

They went to the village inn, and the prince told the innkeeper, in secret, that he was to take away the princess's beautiful dress that night. Next morning the princess had nothing to wear. She was glad when the innkeeper's wife gave her a ragged skirt and an old bodice, and the woman acted as if she were giving her a very fine present. "It's because

your husband is looking after our pigs too, or I wouldn't have done it," she said. "If I gave clothes to everyone who comes to this inn I'd have none left for myself."

So now the princess really believed that her husband was a swineherd, and she was quite sure of it when he took her with him to herd pigs in the nearby mountain pastures for the next few days. However, she worked hard, and when her husband had other things to do she herded the pigs by herself all day without complaining.

She held out for eight days, and then her feet were covered with blisters, and her arms and legs were all scratched by the thistles that grew in the fields. She sat sadly by the stove in the evening, and thought that she couldn't be a good swineherd, for she did not like the pigs.

That evening, when she was alone in the room at the inn where she and the prince were staying, some men came and asked if she knew who her husband really was.

Of course she did. "He is the swineherd of this village," she said, "but he isn't at home just now, for he is a pedlar too, and today he is out selling pins, needles, laces and other things in the village and on the farms. He said it might be late before he came back."

"Come with us," said the men, smiling in a mysterious way, and when she followed them they went ahead of her to the castle and then inside, over broad marble floors and up a magnificent marble staircase to the throne-room above. And there, in the middle of the magnificent hall,

stood a man in an ermine cloak such as kings wear. The swineherd's wife did not know who he was – until he took her in his arms and kissed her.

"You set me such difficult talks, and made me so sad," he whispered, "and now I have made you a little sad for my sake too."

Next day they celebrated their wedding again, and everyone in the country was invited to join the festivities. I wish you and I could have been there as well! The old queen wasn't at the wedding either, for she had been so angry when the prince succeeded in carrying out all her tasks that she sat stiff as a poker in her castle and couldn't move at all. The magnificent festivities lasted three days, and after that the prince and princess lived happily together for many, many years.